The House of Balthus

The House of Balthus

David Brooks

For Richard

"Son of the House of Balthus" is going to be another thing again! A little fibro shack, I imagine — all I can afford.."

take care

ALLEN & UNWIN

David

29.8.04

Copyright © David Brooks 1995

All rights reserved. No part of this book may be reproduced or transmitted in any form or by any means, electronic or mechanical, including photocopying, recording or by any information storage and retrieval system, without prior permission in writing from the publisher.

First published in 1995.
This edition published in 1996 by
Allen & Unwin Pty Ltd
9 Atchison Street, St Leonards, NSW 2065 Australia
Phone: (61 2) 9901 4088
Fax: (61 2) 9906 2218
E-mail: 100252.103@compuserve.com

National Library of Australia
Cataloguing-in-Publication entry:

    Brooks, David, 1953—.
        The house of Balthus.

    ISBN 1 86448 121 8

    I. Title.

A823.3

Set in 11/16 pt Janson Text by DOCUPRO, Sydney
Printed by Australian Print Group, Maryborough, Victoria

10 9 8 7 6 5 4 3 2 1

To my parents
at last
in loving memory
and to Nicolette again

Contents

I. Prologue   1
II. The House of Balthus   15
    The Garden of Worldly Delights
    The Plank
    The Orangery
III. Epilogue   191

Acknowledgements

Many people have helped during the evolution of this book, with small points of information and sometimes a great deal more. I dare not try and list them, in part for fear of leaving someone out, and in part for fear of implicating someone in a project they might not themselves have chosen to join, but I do wish to acknowledge help, and considerable inspiration, and my own great indebtedness.

Prologue

ANOTHER night of insomnia, the fourth, subsiding near dawn into sleep and a vivid dream: a house that is and is not this house, an argument, the hot rooms, faces I know and do not know, and all too soon, with the shower, the first sips of coffee, rinsed away with the other, easier darkness. Later, leafing through the prints again, I can find nothing of them. But why do I look?

This morning, opposite the painting of André Derain, it is the *Portrait de la Vicomtesse de Noailles*. This woman, in her late twenties or early thirties, wears black, and not without style. A faint sheen to her jacket and skirt suggests velvet or some high-quality, finely cut wool, matched carefully by her shoes. Black shoes, black suit, black hair, with long calves, long-fingered hands, long, slender neck and face like so many pools of light on an arc suggesting a thin crescent moon partly hidden by cloud. She is sitting — in fact it is more relaxed than that, for she leans back slightly, legs extended, ankles crossed — in an alcove, with the edge of a window evident behind her, although the illumination in the painting comes not from the window but from an independent, artificial source. The walls of the alcove are bare, as are the small writing desk beside her and, from what can be seen of it, the low cupboard at her back, its door open. She herself is seated on a plain chair with a wicker seat. Everything about her suggests an elegant austerity. The desk has a slim drawer (it is, perhaps, the same desk as that in *Nature morte*). The drawer, too shallow to contain much other than envelopes, letters, a few sheets of paper, remains closed. There is much that remains closed here. Perhaps this is part of the statement: the bareness, the withdrawal, the small, vivid slash of the scarlet blouse over the right breast. Thinking suddenly of the floor, I look carefully amongst the chair legs, the shadows, the legs of the table, but there is nothing, only the scent of shoe-leather, of dust on the unpolished boards, the faintest trace of silk stocking on a woman's tensing calf.

I do not feel that she will speak, this Vicomtesse, or — opening the drawer, taking out pen and paper — write. She seems instead to be waiting and, while she waits, to have withdrawn, like so many others in these paintings, deep within herself. André Derain, too, in the painting which faces this — a large, deep-jowled man in a heavy, striped dressing-gown — seems merely to have glanced at us (or is it again at a mirror?), his mind elsewhere.

∞

A young girl is playing patience. The light falls from behind her and, her right elbow on a card table, she is leaning into shadow. On the table are an unlit candle in a silver candlestick, and a squat silver goblet. Behind it is a large upholstered chair upon which, barely perceptible in the shadow, are a cushion, an open book (face down) and, resting across the book's spine, an open box. Beneath them, between the chair and table — it is hard to tell what is resting upon what here, so deep is the shadow — appears to be a basket upon the rim of which sit two more books and another, smaller basket.

Books and containers, open and closed. It seems, at first, a simple study of a child, divided diagonally into a complex field of shadow and a simpler, clearer light. But it is not so simple. The table upon which the young girl leans has three legs only, although evidently it stands as if on four. If the fourth, as it may be, is hidden by the girl's right leg and a leg of the stool upon which she kneels, it none the less casts no shadow. As if to confirm our gathering suspicions, there is something strange, too, about the heavy drape above her, in the top left-hand corner, held by no apparent cord or hook, pushed back by an invisible hand. The painter has engaged, surely, in a deliberate *trompe l'oeil*, but the reason is not clear. The girl is trying to make sense of the cards; to make the suits come right. I myself am trying to make sense of the painting. Something, certainly, is missing for all of us — girl, painter, audience. Over and again she goes over the cards. Over and again there is something that will not come right. And again, behind her, the striped wallpaper, the bars of a cage.

Months later, coming back to this painting, I notice details I had not noticed before. The girl has only one card in her hand. The game is almost out. And the candle, which I had earlier thought unlit, I see now to be in fact so carefully placed against a pale stripe of the wallpaper that one cannot, having noticed this, dismiss the possibility that it is indeed burning, like the girl herself, with a clear, white, almost invisible flame.

La rue (1933–35) is clearly a revision of *La rue* (1929). The same street corner, the same angle of vision, several of the same key figures: the young man standing self-consciously in the foreground with his hand on his heart; the workman in white crossing the street just behind him, carrying on his shoulder a plank obscuring his face; the man — a wooden cut-out, a sign? — in a chef's hat, standing stiffly on the curb; the woman on the other side, walking away.

Many others, however, have been dropped or replaced. The man in the dark coat who had been crossing the road leading a young boy and girl in sailor suits has become now two adolescents grappling ambiguously before a restaurant window, and the several other conservatively hatted and coated men who, silhouetted in the background or depicted on the panel above the shop on the corner, had seemed to echo him have also disappeared. But why have these men — I find myself calling them the fathers — been removed?

It may be that one of the two children being led across the road has simply shifted, in the second painting, to the far side of the picture to be carried by the retreating woman — for she now holds not the red-smocked girl but a young boy in a sailor suit — and that the other, the girl, is now a toddler chasing a red ball with a blue racquet. Three other figures, however, are quite new. One, in the foreground, is a woman in black with her back to us, just mounting the curb. The others are those juveniles, a boy and a girl, she running, or attempting to, and he, behind her, clasping her to him, his right hand forming a fist and thrust toward the base of her belly, his left gripping her wrist. A game? An assault? The expressions on their faces — on anyone's — give little away.

Immediately after the portrait of Joan Miró and his daughter and painted in the same year is a picture of Thérèse dreaming. Leaning back in a chair, her hands behind her head, her eyes closed as she basks in the warm sunlight streaming through the window, the cat, at her feet, licking at a saucer of milk. Toward the upper left-hand corner, balancing the cat in the composition, are another chair and one end of a table upon which are three empty vases and a crumpled white cloth. Thérèse has her right foot on the floor, her left raised on a footstool. Her red skirt and fresh white petticoat are thrown back and her legs and underwear are fully, if apparently unconsciously, exposed. It is to these that the eyes are first drawn, as much by their uncommonness as subject as by their position within the picture's golden triangle — and to the small, dark stain that might as readily be a scuff in the canvas, a place where the paint has prematurely cracked or become discoloured.

And yet how much of this is not Thérèse dreaming, but the viewer? How much of this is not her reverie but my own? The 'warm sunlight streaming,' the 'cat ... licking at a saucer of milk,' the 'fresh white petticoat,' even 'the picture's golden triangle' — is this the only way of saying such things? Would it be hers?

∞

The titles can be quite misleading. As the editors of this catalogue admit, they are not always the artist's own. It is hard to know how far one should take them.

This, for example, called *La victime*: is its title a misnomer, or a serious signification? It is of a slim girl, olive-skinned, lying —

laid out? — on a white sheet. Do the words indicate that the girl is dead? The swart colour of the skin might well be a corpse's colour, but her pose seems erotic: her left arm placed casually beside her, her right thrown over her head, she has been posed like a lover, or at least to suggest the languor of someone after the act itself. The victim and the vanquished have become confused. Is this a confession — on whose part? — or an attempt to expose a crime? And, if so, is the murder, if that is what it is, a literal or a metaphoric one?

Who is this girl? Where has she come from? And in what sense is she *victime*? Will another painting offer a clue? Or has this artist, this controversial painter of erotic, prepubescent children, simply posed a model in this way to admit his own complicity — to confess some violation which, every time he turns to his favourite theme, he perpetrates upon a wider sensibility, a realm from which he feels himself exiled?

Without changing the given title, without denying her victimness, I find myself wanting to call her the drowned woman. I can see no evidence of violence on her body: there is no welt about her neck, there are no cuts or puncture marks upon her wrists, breasts, belly. There is no sign of blood. Perhaps she has been poisoned; perhaps she has been shot or stabbed in some part not visible to me. I call her the drowned woman partly because only death by water could leave her so smooth and brownly immaculate. Partly, too, it is because of the dusk which, as I watch, is creeping over her like a tide — the currents of darkness that, as she lies on the sheet (pearled, as it is, like an abalone shell), stroke about her thighs, her neck, or seem to comb out straight the long dark hair beside her outflung arm. But mainly it is because, presented in this way — naked, enigmatic, mixing inextricably a sexual invitation with the repulsion of death — something else of her has become submerged beneath her painted form. There is also a she who can not be seen, can not be shown, who has drowned, or may do, beneath all and whatever it is that has produced this image.

Weeks later I return to the painting and am shocked to find, in the deep shadow on the floor beneath her, the faint yet unmistakable outline of a knife. I examine her body again carefully but still there is no wound, nor any sign of blood on the sheet. It is as if someone had come while I was away and tampered with the scene, planting evidence, attempting to influence my conclusions, and of course such a thought is ludicrous. Yet nothing else changes; nothing that has been thought becomes unthought. Even if, as seems undeniable, the knife has been there all the time, it remains only one person's gesture, an idea, a possibility only.

⌔

I turn a page — disquieting, how easy an act this is! — and I am facing the deep perplexity of *La chambre*. A young girl reclines on a sofa. But for her long white socks, her slippers, she too is naked. One leg is stretched across the floor toward the large window at the right. The other, raised and flexed, rests on a pouffe. Her right arm also is extended, thrown back like her head, and her left, presumably bent at her side, is invisible but for the hand resting at the base of her belly. Her eyes are closed as if in sleep or daydream. It is a vision which might bring to one's senses the ethereal strains of Donizetti or the remote, dark scent of roses, but such things are held back by the other figure in the painting, a small, imp-like being who is thrusting aside the rich, heavy curtain to flood the scene with that very light which, I suddenly realise, has been giving it to me. Eyes set close together, nose and chin pointed, she seems to glower at the sleeper, her expression and the posture of her body suggesting malice, anger, disdain. Who is she? Why does she thrust the drape aside? Is she trying to wake the girl or to expose her? But perhaps she is not opening the drape at all. Perhaps she is closing it.

There is also a third figure, a white cat in the far corner, perched on a table beside the window, half in shadow. Its face, too, is pointed, its eyes close together. It seems at first to be looking toward the imp-like figure at the window, but it may be that it looks at us. This painting, like so many of the others, is full of questions, or the provocation of them; full of latent narrative. Perhaps that is why, on the plain wooden table with the high, thin legs, the cat is sitting on a book.

∞

Thèrése rêvant, *La chambre*, the portrait of the Vicomtesse: in the silent intervals of our relationship, the mind, the emotions, a thousand receptors of the memory grope for invisible wires, impalpable threads, as if deep within the world of these paintings as within that beyond them were a web that might connect what has never so far been connected, its strings marked or buoyed by the least prepossessing of objects or the colours or lines that denote them. Finding them, lingering over detail after detail, following as best I can, with whatever patience and delicacy can be mustered, it is as if I were inching in pitch darkness over terrain I have no idea of, guided not by a safety-rope but by the thinnest, most fragile of strings. Often they break or lead nowhere. Sometimes they lead to another painting. Sometimes they branch, or join others. There are even occasions when, following — with eyes as subtle, with fingers as delicate as I am capable of making them — what could almost be described as a nerve of air, I find myself passing through the painted surface, entering the landscape beyond, striking out across the thick wet grass or new-ploughed fields with a consciousness, a purpose other than my own, into a history and geography far from the scene. I wake, these times, from my dream or reverie knowing that I have just been staring at a face or contemplating an object not to be found anywhere in these works at hand — that could not possibly have been, since it is part of the landscape of my self: a crumpled handkerchief that has still upon it the hot, sour-sweet smell of my mother's breath or the dark smear of her lipstick; a marble ashtray that has in it, still gleaming, an acrid mixture of tar and spittle knocked from my father's pipe.

∽

Alice (1933) wears only a chemise and a pair of slippers. One foot up on a chair beside her, she is combing her hair, staring toward the viewer with an abstract gaze that reminds me disconcertingly of the vacant eyes of classical Greek statuary or the *yeux glauques* of a Burne-Jones beggar maid. The task she performs, like her state of undress, suggests that she is alone and that what she is actually staring at, in the invisible plane between us, is a mirror. The Looking Glass, then, but on which side of it *is* she, and from which side am I watching her? Is it she who looks out from the back-to-front world of paradox and nonsense, or is it I?

The ambiguity is supported by the impossibility of telling the original Alice from what might well be only her reflected image — the impossibility of telling whether what I am offered here is the Alice who looks into the mirror, or the girl whom she finds looking back at her — and the corresponding, extraordinary possibility that, if this *is* the mirror surface (since this is what I see when I look into it), *I* am also somehow this girl.

But I am not being entirely honest here. The story the mind tells is not necessarily the story of the eye. What first drew my attention to the painting — what most held it there and called it back — was not at all the intellectual implications of the subject. It was the girl's sex, her cleft, her cunt; to see it, almost at the centre of the picture, not, as in so many of the other works, as a vague area of shadow, but with, so clearly defined, the line where the lips meet, the distinctive slight welling of the flesh, the particular, tender concavity high on the inner thigh, exactly as it is when the leg is opened thus; these, and the meticulous attention to the furniture, the skirting boards, the lie of light on the bent wood, its honeyed fall.

∞

Where does Thèrése go after her warm dream in the sunshine? Where does Derain go? The Vicomtesse de Noailles, in all probability, thanks the artist for the sitting — or is it he who thanks her? — and, changing from the sombre black he has especially asked for, and looking with apprehension and surprise upon the emerging portrait, moves off to her next engagement, wearing one of the latest creations of Christian Dior, about her neck and at her wrist the diamonds from Cartier for which she is so famous, her pleasure at being painted by such an artist mixed with some puzzlement as to whether it is a part of herself — darker, more pensive than she is used to — coming into being beneath his brushstrokes, or whether it is instead a dream, a need of his own. She looks forward with curiosity to the finished work (he has said that she need not sit again) and to the comments of friends when at last she has it in her drawing room: what will they think of the splash of scarlet, the strange posture he has asked her to adopt? What will they think of the bare surroundings, the uncharacteristic dress?

But there is also another, a different Vicomtesse. There is also she who, coming to herself after a moment's absorption (or is it exhaustion — and how long *has* she been sitting there?), rises in the bare room and goes to the window, or moves off toward another part of the apartment, invisible to us, or does not rise at all, but reaches into a pocket or to the floor beside her for a cigarette, lights it, and continues to think, smoking quietly. She whose clothes are these clothes. Whose room is this room. Whose life is this life, continuing beyond this frame.

∞

A grey day. Persistent rain. The pages of this and every other book soft with damp. The eyes of the model in the background of the portrait of André Derain are cast aside, as are those of la Vicomtesse. Thérèse in the 1938 painting looks bored, and in the 1936 painting even depressed. In *Jeune fille au chat* the eyes of the girl are again averted, as they are in *La jupe blanche*, and in neither is she presented as alert or amused. And so, in painting after painting, for years yet, although there are signs later that things change. Can it be that not all who are in the house of these paintings — the house that all of these settings compose — wish to be there? It has become almost customary, when talking about these works, to speak of 'reverie', of 'dream', or of the idyllic world of childhood. If the apparent distraction or boredom of the models has been mentioned, it has been as that of those who are suspended between worlds, no longer fully children, not yet adult, waiting with a smouldering impatience for the blooming, the coming of the body. But the loss, today, on these bored or despondent faces seems to outweigh anticipation. There is even a kind of anger or belligerence in the set jaws. As if the anticipation were far more in those who view them than in the models themselves, or they were already mourning something that the adult world, when it arrives, is likely to submerge entirely. They have the look of prisoners. But whose assumption is it that release will come?

Much later in the volume are the two paintings of the *Japonaise*. In the first, on all fours, she stares into a black mirror set up on a low table beside a large black chest. In the second, again stretched out upon a rug, she stares into a much larger mirror and presumably sees, along with her reflection, the bright red table behind her that occupies so much of the picture-space. But what else does she see? Her eyes, in each painting, are intent upon her own reflection, but although in each case her face can be seen quite clearly, it is just as clear that it is not this, or not only this, that she is looking for. The effect is complicated. Seeing her search beyond or within her own image as she does, I too search further.

It is also, of course, as if she is looking critically at the very things — her face, her figure — at which the viewer too is looking, signalling her awareness that the living form, as well as its representation within the picture, is a created, a painted thing, existing as much to signify what is *not* here as are the closed black chest beside the black mirror, the lidded jar on the bright red table.

The House of Balthus

The Garden of Worldly Delights

1

TWO a.m., and the whole house awakened by knocking. At least, it is difficult, for those who find themselves listening, to imagine how anyone could not be disturbed. Why won't somebody answer the door? Why won't this person realise that they are not welcome, that there is no one to let them in? Why don't they go away?

Winds do not often penetrate the courtyard. Not many winds could. But there are winds and winds. Tonight the leaves of the lemon tree rustle continuously and bend in inexplicable unison, as if a wind were blowing through, not over, the east wing, or the house were not there at all. And outside, on rue Thélin, something similar: not a high wind, perhaps not even a wind truly — it has hardly a strength worth mentioning — but an aged and exhausted listlessness. Papers, leaves drift past, and dust, that seem to have been drifting eternally, from the farthest corners of the world.

Some of the papers carry news, although, with the grey moonlight, the slow, dry turning over gutters and cobblestones, whether it is old news or recent would be hard to tell. Now and then, from one of them, a face looks out — a cleric, a politician, a victim of crime — and seems to search the windows. If it sees anything, however, it does not stop or in any way register the fact. Or perhaps it is that — catching, as surely some of these faces must, the sight of Mme Lecault through her partly opened curtain (it is the eleventh night), biting down on absolute desolation or panic — it has something like mercy.

The knocking continues. Various tenants rise and go to their courtyard windows, open their curtains slightly, peer through. But no, there is no one, or the angle is such that they cannot see. Only the dry scrape of the lemon tree, only the leaves. There are brief intervals, sometimes of several minutes or more, when they might almost allow themselves to think that the person has gone away, but over and again it resumes, patternless, angry, imploring. Eventually, one by one, they come to the conclusion that it is not in the courtyard after all — though for a time it had certainly sounded like that — nor even anything to do with this house, but somewhere out in the street, at the building next door perhaps, or the building beyond that, brought to them the more loudly and clearly by this unusual wind. Somewhere someone's lapdog — it is that kind of sound — barks and is shut up. A little later someone opens a window and shouts. More than one tenant contemplates donning a dressing-gown and putting on slippers to go out and find the person, to beg or to order them to stop, but at the thought of a possible scene or worse (it is not only Mme Lecault who remembers the story of Gaston Foch) gives up the idea.

And still the knocking continues, stopping, then starting again, angry, defeated, importunate. An eternity, even if it is only an hour or more. Perhaps, indeed, that is what it is. The wind, with its knuckles bleeding. A shutter. A loose board. The ghost of a madman. Eternity.

2

The Countess sleeps with her disease, her knees clenched tight. She feels her blue blood bruised, contagion breaking out upon it like potato-mould. She dreams, in what dreams she remembers, that she is running headlong over darkened fields, her outstretched arms bound to a staff behind her and her hands aflame, her blazing fingers brushing the tinder of the waiting pyres, leaving in her wake a night full of crowding screams, a night full of burning women. She cannot help it. Nothing she can do can stop it. Lurching to avoid one pyre she reels into another.

Sometimes, in a different dream, it is she who is tied, not to a stake but to a twisted tree. No wood is stacked about her, and it is her mouth alone that burns, the small, tenacious flames clinging to her lips, her tongue, every scream, every word, every panicked or exhausted exhalation fanning them.

Stars appear. Watching herself thus, from a position outside herself, only a short way off in the darkness, she sees in the sky above her a hand, a tongue, a monstrous eye, a great tear falling from it, several large crows. It is midnight, or perhaps long after, in her narrow bed, to a rasping from across the courtyard, tinder dry, that may be a window closing, a match drawn slowly over a paving stone.

3

Blood, he had said, in a rich, heavy accent, but with a voice that struggled through phlegm, the tips of his ancient fingers almost knocking over the crystal glass with their shaking. Big fingers that had been rough and dry and hard when Michael had been forced to shake hands with him and everyone had laughed, nervously. The old man had held his hand too long, as if he had forgotten he was doing it, still moving it up and down while he was talking about something else.

Frogs, he said then, and Michael had been surprised and thought that he was trying to be funny, that perhaps he should laugh. But he had looked up and everyone was so serious, as if there were something serious about frogs, as if frogs were no laughing matter.

Vermin. The deep red drops splashing on the stiff white cloth, suddenly like a little crowd of vermin — mice, maybe, or cockroaches — scattering out amongst the dinner plates before coming to rest, sinking.

Boils, the ragged voice louder and softer at the same time, the gnarled head when you looked at it — were you supposed to? — like a giant's on an old bird's body, a crow's or a buzzard's, a vulture's, one of those birds that hovers over the dying and the dead ...

Darkness. More phlegmy still, barely able to get the words out through whatever thickness was stopping them, but the fresh drops still coming, dark and concentrated, glistening amongst the paler, older, widening ones, like something, suddenly, he could and couldn't remember, on the edge of his mind, in the dark there, thick and red and shining, making him feel clammy and unstable, as if someone were tilting his chair, mother and father not touching their own glasses, looking on respectfully, confusedly. At home it was bad if someone spilt wine. Mother would rush to get towels and cloths from the kitchen, and then would pile salt on it, right to its very edges.

Then something had happened. Michael could not tell what. At first he thought it was himself but it was not. Suddenly the old man was making deep, rasping sounds and had his hands up over his face, pushing his funny little skull-cap crooked, and the two thin ladies, his daughters, were getting up and bumping the table, and their beads were rattling, and their thin hands were shaking and leading him away, mother too, leaving him and his father sitting there and the old man's glasses resting on the spotted cloth, focusing the light into two sharp points like tiny comets, a red drop trickling down one of the lenses and his father saying It's alright, it's alright, more often than he needed, amidst the plates and the crystal and the, what was it called, Seder dish, as if trying to convince himself, fumbling for his pipe which he couldn't light there anyway, which mother had told him he couldn't, and which, Michael could tell, had already made him angry with her.

It is one of the earliest things. He could not have been five. It is the blood that reminds him, the blood and the feathers, probably of the pigeon he was watching yesterday. It had been trying to fly but could only flutter loudly, and rise a few inches, and veer away to the right, landing no more than a metre or two from where it had started. Always to the right, so that it would eventually finish the circle.

Always there is something that people are not telling, or something that they can't. Always something that you are not told. How many plagues were there? Trying to count them, saying over the ones he remembers, flicking his fingers, spattering the flagstones with invisible wine ...

4

The postman, M. Rocquart, delivers the mail directly to Mme Lecault, who then sorts it herself into the tenants' pigeonholes. It's a long-standing arrangement, and has rarely been queried. It saves M. Rocquart time — which he often spends in drinking a cup of tea with Mme Lecault — and, as she likes to think of it, helps her keep track of the tenants, and so to do what is best for the house, which is always (as she tells herself in periods of particular awkwardness or when she does discover something untoward) more than the sum of its residents. To be forewarned is to be forearmed.

Certainly there are things that she has found out in this way that the tenants themselves might not have told her. That the Countess, for example, has a lover — or at least that she receives, with a regularity that such a relationship might explain, letters from a M. Dufort in Brussels — neat, beautifully typed envelopes of an expensive kind, addressed not to 'Countess', but simply, affectionately — intimately? — to 'A. de Montrecourt'. Or that Mme Barber's husband is not English, as that lady has claimed, but Italian, and still alive, and moves a great deal about France, Italy and Spain, a set of facts at which Mme Lecault has arrived by careful process of deduction, having just the once, as an experiment, placed in Mme Barber's pigeonhole a letter, strangely redirected, addressed not to Mme Madelaine Barber, but to Mme Madelena Radnotti, vaguely remembering that a letter to a gentleman of that surname had been returned to Mme Barber some months before, undeliverable as addressed. Mme Lecault is certain, moreover, that these slim envelopes — too slim for letters — are cheques or money orders, since Mme Barber does not work, and since her rent is paid, sometimes several weeks in arrears, almost always just after these letters arrive. Perhaps Radnotti is a fugitive, or a traveller with a bad conscience, though it is hardly Mme Lecault's business to jump to conclusions.

The writer, too, she has learnt something about. A strange man, absent-minded, much of his correspondence comes from a publisher in Paris, and as much again from a literary agent there. Often, too, there are packages of books, some of them very large and heavy packages. Mme Lecault deduces from this that he is perhaps more well-known than he lets on. On the one or two occasions she has visited a bookstore to find out, no one seems to have heard of him, but surely this only confirms the fact. Isn't it true that many writers — the greatest, anyway — do not use their real names? Certainly he too does not seem to have any other employment, but has never wanted for money — has always paid his rent on time, and dines at good restaurants far more often than most could afford.

The painter, Miklus, on the other hand, she knows is quite infamous, at least in a small way. He receives mail from many people, and some of the names she recognises from the newspapers — other artists, writers, even a university teacher who was once in trouble over a pamphlet he had written. A little like the Professor, who also seems to be important in his own circle, and who receives mail, often fat, tattered letters, from several different countries — Morocco, Australia, Canada, Paraguay, Réunion — and as often from exotic-sounding universities as from friends in the monastic order he has told her he once belonged to (and which she suspects defrocked him).

The other tenants rarely receive anything of much interest. M. Christophe regularly gets a letter from his dead wife's mother, and sometimes from members of his own family — a brother in Lyons, or his elderly parents in Saint Bastien. Much like the Blochs, M. and Mme Ségur receive family mail, bills, and ladies' magazines (Mme Lecault imagines most of his mail must go to his office), and the Pizacs, like Auguste, receive very little at all (Pizac himself, she suspects, could hardly string two sentences together although Marguerite is intelligent enough, and Auguste is illiterate and proud of it).

She never steams open the letters. At least, not any longer. Not since the day she opened one particular letter, after which she could not do it again. There is a limit, after all, to what one should know of another.

5

Although friendly enough with Miklus, and known to have held long conversations with Mme Lecault (chiefly about food), the Professor is not much given to talking with his neighbours, but will frequently disturb and not infrequently charm them by playing loud music on his gramophone, chiefly the symphonies of Gustav Mahler and Anton Bruckner, the operas of Richard Wagner, and an eccentric miscellany of arias sung by the great tenors and sopranos. He has a weakness, too, for the music of Heitor Villa Lobos, and in particular — his greatest favourite — the Bachianas Brazileiras, at the end of her great recording of the fifth of which Victoria de los Angeles strikes a long, high note so pure, so clear, so preternaturally stable that he has sometimes felt, at the very back of his skull, something straining quite tangibly for the infinite.

He has been known to drink a good deal, and there has always been, at the end of the week, a small collection of bottles — mostly brandy bottles, although sometimes, too, a greenish, age-clouded bottle bearing a label upon which the words Romaneé Conti or Clos Vougeot are prominent — beside his garbage bin in the service lane on the east side of the house. Recently, however, with a mild heart attack now behind him, he has been urged to restrict himself to mineral waters, and although he has never taken the advice very seriously, the insipid, clear-glass necks of such bottles intersperse the thicker brown or elegant green shoulders of the others, adding an element of drab conformity to his garbage.

He is a big man, for he eats a great deal — this, too, he has been warned about, but one can only give up so much at a time — and at least once a fortnight, in addition to his own market shopping, there is what many would see as an immoderate consignment of delicacies delivered to him from a leading delicatessen in the centre of the town. Although they are rarely encouraged to talk to him — although they may have tried on such occasions and found him apparently deaf and blind to them — the other tenants can see him almost every evening, just before sunset, sitting inside his large front window, staring out intently toward the centre of the courtyard.

At the centre of the courtyard is a small lemon tree. Sometimes, toward the end of a long afternoon, when the wine and the music have become increasingly interfused, the Professor begins to imagine that the shadow of the lemon tree on the small patch of lawn is his own lost soul coming back, and that, if he were ever, at one of these moments, to walk over to the lemon tree — as he longs to do — and step into the cool, soft shadow beneath it, he would drop suddenly into nothingness and keep on falling. But this fear in itself is not what stops him. It is really only half his fear. The other half — the other fear — is that nothing would happen, that it is not his soul at all.

6

Mirrors are magical, though it is almost impossible to catch them at their most marvellous. Coming upon the ornate silver hand-mirror face down on his mother's dressing-table at the age of three or four, and forbidden as he had been to touch anything there, Michael had been unable to resist lifting it, at first gingerly, by the very edge, and then, after several initial attempts had failed (the process took some time since, as he reasoned it, you would have to leave at least a day between each try, to allow the timid image to reappear), snatching it up by the handle, to see if his mother's face were still in it. Also a failure usually, though perhaps not always, for there were occasions when something was caught momentarily before fleeing to the edges as if, for the merest, fleeting second it had been dazzled by the sudden light.

Although he himself could never have put it that way, it was in the mirror, too, that he had found the first solid evidence of something else he had come to suspect, for it had not been long before, attempting thus to catch what might have been, what *must* have been left there, he discovered that everything reflected was in fact reversed, as if it were not the real world that you saw at all, but some sort of inside-outness, especially on the day when, having begun to learn to read, he held up to the mirror his favourite story to discover that within each word — even the words he had thought he had mastered — was a hidden word, a strange, secret writing.

The two notions, after all, seemed clearly to support each other. If mirrors turned things back-to-front, then surely there was just some chance they did it to time also. Looking into it, in any case, he would sometimes almost drown himself, before coming out on the other side, and if he had not seen his mother there, moving palely, faintly behind or within his own face, he had definitely seen a self, a Michael, that he could never see otherwise, a self that *was* himself, that was always with him, wherever he went, but that, he became increasingly sure, no one else could ever see.

Perhaps it was this, his mother's other, secret self, he had been looking for all along, a self he had once, long ago, seen looking down at him, as if he himself had been a mirror that she held.

7

On the wall of one of the upstairs rooms, a room that is always darkened, a room upon which the curtains are never opened, there is a large engraving of an old but massive and powerful man with a straight back, broad shoulders and a huge white beard below voluminous white hair. His face is deeply lined and his large eyes are piercing and authoritative. One of the patriarchs, certainly, but perhaps no one of them in particular. The engraving is so detailed that it might be a photograph, and yet the details are so archetypical that they might belong to any century. He is wearing long black robes and sitting half turned away from a desk upon which there are a huge book and a candlestick. From the shadows about him — for the only light there is comes from the candle — there protrude scrolls and obscure folds of some priestly vestments. His robes fall open from one shoulder to expose one half of his chest, and there is suggested the unexpectedly soft, pale skin of the aged. Only a portion of this, however, is visible, for held across his chest, cradled in one arm (his right hand holds a quill), is a small child. The child's face is not visible and there is nothing about it — no symbolic vestment — to suggest particular identity. The child's head, in fact, is turned away from the viewer. The old man — the patriarch — is giving suck.

The engraving, in a heavy and darkly-varnished frame, hangs above a desk not unlike the desk that it depicts. Upon this desk, the real desk, are a small reading lamp, a pen, and one large book, lying open. A bookshelf, an armchair, a threadbare carpet — there is little else in the room. The book is a journal or manuscript of some kind. The paper, at the point where it has been opened, is white, fresh, newly written. A few loose sheets of paper can be made out around the feet of the desk, some of them partially covered with a small, neat hand. When one's eyes grow more accustomed to the dimness, one can also make out, on the left, a heavily-curtained window and, on the right, even deeper in shadow, a large, panelled door, heavier and more imposing than one would expect from the rest of the house, as if it belonged to a different time or had a function quite unlike any other. For those who return to the room — and return is not always possible — to ponder the engraving or attempt to decipher the text written in so small a hand, it is this, the door, which ultimately and inexplicably exercises the greatest attraction.

8

Mme Lecault could tell you a great deal about most of the tenants of the house, but there are exceptions. The young couple, for instance: the pair she has come to think of as the Lovers. She has rules about such things, and is almost certain that they break them, but there was something about them when they first appeared that made her believe them, if not for what they said (it was the thinnest, least plausible of stories) then for what they were, and prevented her from asking for the usual papers. She had been trapped, almost, and more or less by herself, with an ease that might have puzzled or bemused her if she didn't trust so well her own instincts, or feel in this instance so strangely confident. M. Valle's affairs — that awful business — had only just been settled, and although it had never taken her so long before, there had not been time to think carefully enough through the matter of a new tenant. From hints that Auguste had dropped she had felt sure he was going to offer the rooms — which had an entrance opposite his own and, unlike the rest of the apartments, were reached not from the courtyard but from an outside staircase at the rear of the building — to one of his wine-drinking, card-playing, smelly and doddering friends without asking her, and so forcing her to say yes or no, either of which answers would mean even less work out of him than she now got. So the couple had seemed, at the time, a simple way out. She had let them have the room for a month only, while they found work and looked for another and less expensive lodging, but they had been so quiet, and *so* like that couple in *The Necklace* (or like those wild children in the English book that had made her cry so much), and there had been no sign of the raised eyebrows she had half expected from the Blochs or Ségurs. Indeed it seemed as if the aura that they had had about them when they first appeared at her door — a warm, wet, pathetic thing that had made her think of half-drowned kittens, wet sparrows — had either served to make them more or less invisible, or worked the same charm on all the others in the house.

And, yes, beautiful: there was something beautiful about them both. Darkly and sadly. Incipient death, perhaps, which you could sometimes see, and that may have been why she had not wanted to ask. His fine, pale features and piercing eyes; her long and lifeless black hair. She knew only that their names were Paul and Justine, that they had come from the country, and that, supposedly, they were M. and Mme Celle, or Celé, or Ciel — she had not caught it properly when she had first been told, and was anyway so sceptical about their status that it hardly mattered. They were more like brother and sister. Perhaps to others as much as to herself. And perhaps that was why they had caused so little comment. (Although a brother and sister, sharing the one room. . .) But it was not that. Some people are attracted only to those who look somehow like them. Others grow to look more and more alike the longer they are together. That old couple one sometimes saw shopping on the rue Richelieu, so alike they could exchange their clothes and you might not tell: him letting his white hair get longer and her cutting hers, and carrying the same string bags, and with the same peaked noses and tight wrinkled faces, the same stoop, and the strange way that, looking back at you, they made you feel — as if you knew a secret, and knew that you knew, but could not remember what the secret was.

But it was also, with this Paul and Justine, that one saw so little of them. They had paid the first month's rent on the day they arrived, and the money for a second — no word having been spoken — appeared in an envelope under her door a month later to the day. It had occurred to Mme Lecault that accepting this had amounted to an agreement of a sort, but beyond concluding that one or another of them had found work she had thought no more about it. Probably shift work, since when they were seen it was only at the oddest hours, looking ever paler and thinner, as if neither ever slept well (or, quite the opposite, as if both slept too much). The windows and curtains of their upstairs room were rarely opened, even in the hottest weather, and only late at night or in the earliest hours of the morning did one see the glow of a light behind them. Once there had been some muffled shouting, but it had been in the middle of a weekday and there had been almost no one else in the building. Once, too, concerned after having seen nothing at all of them for a week or more, she had gone to their door and knocked. Paul had answered, after a long time, in a heavy dressing-gown, and it had been as if she had woken him from the sleep of the dead. The room behind him was in a tomb-like darkness yet there had issued from it a fresh and fragrant smell, a smell with almost a winter chill within it, quite the opposite of the rank hothouse vapours she had only then realised she had been expecting. She had muttered a few apologetic words — that she had been concerned, that she had not seen them — and had thought to ask him to come down to see her when he found it convenient, but had wondered afterward whether he had remembered at all that she had come. Certainly he had never appeared at her door; at least not yet.

9

On the west side the Countess, the Professor, and in the small north-western apartment Madelaine Barber and her daughter

Catherine; on the north side the writer Augustine Bernard and the Blochs and, in the two facing apartments over the stairwell Auguste the gardener and the Lovers; on the east the Christophes, the Ségurs and, in the long attic studio above them, overlooking the many-chimneyed, grimy roofs of the nearby buildings, but also catching the unimpeded morning light, the aerial passageways of cats and the ceaseless traffic of the doves, the artist Miklus; on the south, on either side of the main entrance, Mme Lecault herself and the Pizacs. The design, loosely, four wings about a courtyard, the east, south and west part of the original building, their apartments, although tall and narrow and representing various subdivisions of the older house, of a certain spacious elegance, while the north, being a gradual enclosure of the once-separate farm-workers' quarters and storage spaces, has a warren-like quality. Narrow alleyways on the east and west sides allow rear access to several apartments, although for the most part entrance is through the enclosed arch on the south side, by Mme Lecault's, and thence by individual front doors off the courtyard.

The oldest inhabitant is Auguste, the gardener (seventy-four), followed, by just over half a decade, by the Professor, then closely by Mme Lecault. The youngest is Mara Pizac, six months behind Stéphane Christophe, who is nine. The earliest resident Auguste again, followed by the Ségurs and Mme Lecault (the previous concierge, as Auguste tells it, having died of apoplexy while screaming at a German officer in the Place des Basques); the most recent the couple with a name like the sky.

But already there are problems, qualifications. Behind the present tenants there are those of the past — M. Valle the watchmaker, the old woman who used to be an opera singer, the strange spinster sisters who disappeared with less than a day's notice on the advice of a Burmese spiritualist, the retired inspector of police who went to live in Tahiti with his illegitimate daughter, the young boy who was murdered just inside the street entrance by Gaston Foch on his rampage, and many, many others. Old arguments, secrets, pain lodged in plaster cracks, gaps in the grouting, thoughts and dreams and obsessions that have left oblique shadows, stains in the air, harder and softer passages in the spaces that the present occupants pass through. Paying tenants, visible architecture represent only a vanguard. Some people, entering a building for the first time, realise they have known it all their lives. Others, although they may live there a decade or more, know almost nothing of it, will always be temporary residents only. And whether temporal or physical, the spaces we occupy, no less than the people we find ourselves occupying them with, are always in some incalculable but potent part spaces we have occupied earlier or people we have known before. There are some who would say that the future, too, has no clothes to wear but those of the present and the past, and so will often be confused with them.

10

Mme Lecault met Mme Berry after twenty-seven nights of insomnia. They would have killed anyone else. Now, in retrospect, it seems to her as if she was called — dragged slowly towards Mme Berry over all the immeasurable dark acres of wakefulness. She had tried almost everything to avoid it — brandy, long walks, counting sheep, reading Balzac, eating little, eating much, herbal remedies, hot baths, self-hypnosis, sleeping-pills, prayer, listening to classical music, the keeping of lists, picturing the waves far out at sea — but nothing had worked.

Then, eventually, sitting up in the armchair by the small reading lamp with an infusion of valerian, staring blankly into the darkness at the end of the room, clutching her woollen shawl with one hand and the spine of *Old Goriot* with the other, the heavy, root smell of the herb rising almost visibly into the dark above her like a calculated invocation, she heard the noises begin, softly and only intermittently at first, in a way that suggested they might have been going on some time before she noticed them: faint rustlings, sounds occasionally identifiable as the clink of crockery or the rattle of pans; at one point the clear shuffle of shoes on stone, at another what she could have sworn was the systematic snapping of carrots, or celery-stalks. And then, on the twenty-seventh night, after the third such occurrence and perhaps twenty minutes after the noises had begun, the tenuous outline of Mme Berry, or rather the person she would later come to know as that lady.

It was some time — another three or four nights — before this happened again, and somewhat longer before the full form appeared, but by this time other things had started to take shape as well, the glint of polished copper, the vague shape of a fireplace, a coalscuttle, a sink, a broom, in what was obviously, if absurdly, a corner of a kitchen at the house-end of the living-room.

After almost a month of insomnia one is not surprised by very much at all. Mme Lecault, in any case, was too exhausted to do anything but watch. There was always the possibility that it was a dream, after all, and that she had simply forgotten what sleep was like. The woman was dressed in a housekeeper's costume of perhaps two or three centuries before. She seemed to be involved in the small, late-night kitchen tasks that one does when one cannot sleep, or while waiting up for some one or thing. Every now and again, in response to the faint tinkle of a bell somewhere above her head, she would walk quite simply and naturally through the solid stone wall to her left, to return a few minutes later with a cup or glass or tray, or to prepare such a thing to take away again. On one occasion, it seemed to Mme Lecault, there were tears in her eyes.

There was no communication. At least, not for several weeks. On a night soon after these first tentative appearances, Mme Lecault found herself able to sleep at last, and it was not until another severe bout of insomnia — not quite as long as before — that she saw Mme Berry again. At first, as on the earlier occasions, she did not seem to be aware of Mme Lecault at all. Eventually, however, on the fourth night of this new period, Mme Lecault detected an increasing slowness and stiffness in the woman's movements, such as might have suggested a growing consciousness of another's presence. The same sort of tasks were performed as before, but this time a little more carefully, more self-consciously. Perhaps, Mme Lecault thought, it was that the woman was now beginning to hear her just as she had earlier begun to hear the woman: quiet as Mme Lecault had always tried to be, there had, of course, been the occasional clearing of the throat, the occasional creaking of the chair or bones, the occasional rustling of clothes or — struggle as one might to restrain it — breaking of wind.

If she was aware of her, however, the woman seemed in no particular haste to depart. Could it have been that she was as interested in Mme Lecault's possibility as Mme Lecault was in hers? As previously, it was only near dawn that she walked through the wall with a tired air of finality, loosening the strings of her cap as she went, the ghost-kitchen fading slowly thereafter with the gradual coming of daylight.

Mme Lecault grew more confident. She resolved on the next night to speak, but was perhaps too sudden, too loud when she did so. The woman stiffened, turned around, and looked long and carefully into all corners of the room. Apparently seeing no one there, she turned again and departed hastily, nervously, and, at least for that night, finally through the wall. On the next night, however, she was there once more, if a little later than on the previous occasions, and Mme Lecault took it as a promising sign. She spoke more softly. The woman, looking long into what seemed as if it must be to her a darkness, at last fixed her gaze in the right direction. 'Who is there?' she asked, and Mme Lecault tried to explain.

11

Lucien Christophe has a bad leg. It is time that he admitted it, although the thought frightens him more than he could ever say, or find anyone to tell. He has had it for at least eight years. He does not know for certain when it began, or what started it, although he has a good idea. One time, before the children were born, he woke in the double bed that he and Madelaine had managed to squeeze into the opened closet alcove in Poitiers, and there were pins and needles down his right side, pins and needles that would not go away. For a week he had tolerated them but then, as he began to trip over things, as he began to lose feeling, he had gone to a doctor and been told that he had most likely pinched a nerve. Returning a week later he had actually fallen while entering the doctor's surgery. He was admitted to hospital for tests.

In the month that he was there the pins and needles turned to a numbness and paralysis that spread gradually to his left leg and then as slowly ebbed away. The doctors had ceased talking about a pinched nerve, but no further, surer diagnosis was made. For two or three years he had seemed to have recovered completely, but then, one day, he and Madelaine had taken an unusually long walk. The weather had been beautiful, the neighbours had offered to look after Thérèse, and they had gone further than they had intended, enjoying the chance to talk. But as they turned back he had stumbled once or twice, then found his right foot dragging. By the time they had reached home he was pronouncedly lame.

It had scared them both, but since neither was accustomed to walking such distances the problem had not recurred for some time. He had managed successfully to push it from his mind until two years later, just after Madelaine had died. An old friend, mindful of his grief, had invited him to bring the children to Carcassonne for a holiday, and on the way they had stopped to visit another, older friend whom he'd not seen in many years. This friend had married since Lucien had seen him, and had had three children much the age of Stéphane and Thérèse. Over lunch he had spoken enthusiastically of the ruins of what he suspected might have been a sun temple on a hillside some two or three kilometres away, and, forgetting his leg, Lucien had agreed to walk over with him to see them. Halfway there the trouble had begun again, and they had had, eventually, to rest every few hundred yards. The friend had joked about how much they had both aged, but in fact they were only in their early thirties. There was no real excuse.

Now it has come back again. For two or three years, if he is honest with himself, it has threatened to do so more and more. If he sleeps badly, or is ill, or has drunk too much, he will find himself limping, his foot less manageable, harder to lift, as if a heavy, invisible weight were attached.

It was Thérèse's birthday that alarmed him. Not the birthday itself, but what had happened that morning as he tried to prepare. She and Stéphane always slept late on Saturdays, and since he had found himself awake at seven he had left them a note, spoken to Mme Lecault, and had gone into the town to buy his daughter a gift. He'd not been able to find what he wanted — a particular book of Italian fairytales — but had become typically fixated. People kept telling him of another place where he might try for it, and he'd found himself far over on the other side of town. The leg hadn't troubled him because he'd stopped so often, but on the long walk back it had become a positive embarrassment. Friends he'd encountered had asked him what was wrong, and he'd had to stop several times to rest. He'd arrived home late, hot, severely distressed, and without the gift. Thérèse had been wonderful — she always was — but the day had been ruined. And since that day, almost three months ago now, the problem has never really gone away. Unless he sleeps well — and he an insomniac! — unless he tempers his exertion, unless he watches his health carefully, it will be there by mid afternoon or early evening, nagging, dragging him downward, the leading dog in a menacing pack that will never let him rest. The dog, as it seems to him at the exhausted end of such days, with grief, with failure on its back.

12

It is almost five, on a morning in midsummer. Somewhere over the roofs, beyond the apartments, a cock is crowing and the thin irregular chorusing of birds has begun. There is a chill in the air, but of the surface only, requiring no more than the light shirt, the long white cotton pants he has been sleeping in. Although there is no one but the cat to wake, the artist, Miklus, moves slowly, carefully, registering — perhaps it is *to* register — each creak of floorboard under his substantial weight, each whisper of hinge or doorlatch, each deep, quiet groaning of a stair on the long, steep flight to the courtyard.

Outside, barefoot on the shallow steps, the ancient paving of the yard, the cool, dry texture of the stone, trodden already a million times seems yet, this morning, trodden only for the first, as the air seems first breathed, the delicate sunlight, like the ants, the tiny lizards, first seen, the rougher stone of the wall and the leaves of the bushes first touched. *I am going somewhere*, he thinks, but there is nowhere to go, no need. Perhaps it was anxiety that woke him, but there is none apparent. Perhaps it was a dream. The long, perfect moments are utterly empty, the light, like the birdsong, thickening minute by minute. *If only I could not think about this*. Paused again on the lip of it. Unable again to slip through.

13

Michael would never have thought they'd be friends, yet the long, listless afternoons of their holidays — the hours when, because of the heat, one must stay indoors with the curtains drawn, and one's parents are working, or asleep, and there is nothing to do but read or listen to the radio, or do puzzles, or play quiet games — seem to have made them so. Somehow, from watching each other furtively from windows, from talking briefly, nervously in the courtyard, from ignoring one another totally at school, as they had been doing for most of the year so far, or seeing each other sometimes with their parents in the town, they have begun to sit about together, playing cards, talking about their friends or the other tenants in the house, comparing indolently the different aspects of their lives.

Somehow, too, Michael has quite thoroughly overcome the slight aversion he had once felt for her. Not really because she was a girl — he had never much been troubled by that — but because of the time, three years ago, at the first test they had ever had, when she had wet herself at the desk in front of him and the whole class had laughed as the angry, embarrassed teacher ushered her from the room. It had never happened again, but for a long time afterward he had associated her with unpleasant, wet sensations, acrid smells. Now, with her lazy playfulness, her sudden, clever, sarcastic comments, her air of knowing about things he'd not yet even thought of, she seemed quite different.

This afternoon they are at her father's apartment (her mother is dead, as his own mother has told him, though she did not say when or how). Michael is crouched on the persian rug, reading one of M. Christophe's war books: he has a whole set, one for each year, and has given Michael permission to read them — even to borrow them — whenever he likes. Thérèse is sitting on the couch. She has been drawing at the table in front of her — a large picture of a cat and a rainbow — but now seems to have fallen asleep. Her eyes, anyway, are closed, and her head is thrown back. Gri-gri, the Christophes' white cat, is sitting, with its eyes closed, barely a metre from them.

The pictures Michael has been looking at — of bodies in ditches, of tanks rolling down streets lined with bombarded buildings, of frightened, exhausted people pushing carts and bicycles loaded down with tiny mountains of possessions, whole households on wheels — make him feel strange and uncomfortable, as if he contains something too large for him, that is pressing outward from within. He has found himself thinking of what it must be like to have a bayonet go through you, or to have a bullet enter your own chest or thigh. Everything — the pictures, the atmosphere of the room — is suddenly oppressive. He would like to talk to Thérèse, to suggest that they go outside or back to his family's apartment, but is not sure whether or how to wake her. He did so once before and she was angry and they fought. It's too hot for that now.

He looks toward her. Under the table he can see her leg up to her knee, and then a long way up, under her dress. She often sits like that, with her hands behind her head, and her eyes closed, and one leg drawn up.

For reasons he's not sure of — perhaps it is only to wake her — Michael reaches over and touches her above the ankle lightly. She does not move. He leaves his hand there for a while, moving it backward and forward slightly, as if all he were really doing were tickling, then slowly moves it up her leg. Still he doesn't quite know why. There is a strange feeling in his pants, a hotness, and his penis is becoming stiff and uncomfortable, but it is important, now, that she not wake, and that he move his fingers as far up her leg as he can. It's a sort of game, he thinks, like sneaking up on somebody, though he's not quite sure, if she doesn't wake up, that he'll tell her he's played it.

When he reaches her knee he has to come closer, and he is sure that the sound of his movement on the rug or his breath so near her leg will wake her, but she still sleeps. Eventually his fingers have moved right up, almost to where her legs join. She scares him for a moment when she moves her left leg slightly, but it is only that, and serves only to open her thighs more widely, and she doesn't move again. He looks across at the cat and sees that it is awake and staring at him, twitching the end of its tail.

He has gone so far now that he might as well continue. It scares him, but it seems to him that her reaction would probably be no different if she were to wake now than if she were to wake when he had gone further, although he is not yet sure what that entails. Something, anyway, seems to be driving him: stopping no longer occurs to him.

For a long time he gently rubs the cotton of her underpants, and then, very slowly and carefully, eases his finger beneath it and around the elastic on the inside of her leg. It is very warm there, and slippery, like the inside of one's cheek. He rubs his finger up and down, up and down, just slightly further each time until, on one of the downward strokes, he encounters the edge of something else — not one of the vertical folds, but tighter, harder. It is like a prearranged signal. As soon as it happens he withdraws his hand, crawls back from the table, and stands up as quietly as he is able, his heart pounding almost painfully. Thérèse, incredibly, is still asleep. The white cat yawns and stretches and, as Michael leaves — remembering at the last second the book he had arranged to borrow — follows him out.

14

Born to Belgian parents in Brazil three nights before the turn of the century, Axel Ségur, now well past fifty, is a dealer in antiques. His modest success in this calling he attributes to his scrupulous professionalism, a slight disinclination toward the objects of his trade having allowed him at all the most important times to keep a cool head and to approach all propositions rationally. His own taste, indeed, leans more toward the Biedermeier, with which he and his wife Hélène have consistently if sparsely furnished their apartment: that, and the considerable matters of his suits, his shoes.

He is, he would have thought, the last person to start seeing angels. Perhaps if his mother had given birth on time, or been able to hold on a few days longer, but she had done so too long already by then, and it had been clearly a part of his obscure and perplexing but none the less definite fate to be born a few minutes before midnight on December the twenty-eighth, 1899, on a tide of blood from a crude and hasty episiotomy, accentuating his arrival — so the embarrassing story had gone — with the largest and blackest spattering of meconium the doctor had ever seen.

This is not to say that he knew nothing about angels, but again it was his objectivity, his scepticism that had marked the acquaintance so far. Indeed, the proudest his cool head had ever been allowed to become had been when, in a palazzo in Perugia, he had discovered some unknown putti by Giovanni Bellini, and there had, ever since, been a steady if never so prestigious trickle of such ikons through his hands — hand-carved wooden angels most often, but sometimes of plaster or porcelain, and on a handful of occasions (it was not his particular forte) angels painted on canvas or on board, but only if there were someone by to verify their pedigree.

How to explain, then, what he had seen on a night when, the full moon shining through a crack in the curtains having troubled his sleep, he had risen to urinate and had happened, penis in hand, to look out through the glass louvres of the toilet window? There, some twelve feet below, near the centre of the courtyard, he had seen the almost-exact image of Thérèse Christophe, except that, at two a.m., mistily transparent, and floating at least a hand's width above the blue-black flagstones, it could have been no such person.

It was exactly the unlikelihood that snared him. There had seemed no point in telling Hélène. He had been afraid of her laughter, amongst other things, since once or twice, and upon far more likely matters, this had been most harsh. But perhaps, had he done so, it might have troubled him less. Laughter might have sent it off, prevented it from gaining a foothold. As it was, it had too quickly gone too far. Not that he had soon seen her again (her, or he: he was no longer sure: might not a male angel also have long hair?), but he had found himself, on nights when he could not sleep, sometimes rising and going to the window. And, not finding the angel again, he'd begun to search for it in books, to mark out possibilities in catalogues, to look for them — for how else is such a dealer to go about such a search? — in auction rooms and old estates.

He encountered less difficulty than he might have thought. One might almost say they sought him out in their turn, or, rather, exercised angelic powers to attract his eye. Never *the* angel, *his* angel, of course, but small china cupids, delicate seraphim of Italian or Bohemian glass, stern, prayerful angels from forgotten graves, carved, gilded putti from rococo cornices. They glanced at him from windows, looked down from eaves, crowded the margins of trecento manuscripts, appeared where he had never recalled seeing them before. He bought several, making of them something of a specialty, and more and more he found them difficult to part with, the professional objectivity in which he'd so long taken pride crumbling before an unexpected, gentle covetousness.

It troubled him. Not only the loss of objectivity — though that did too — but what it might stand or stand in for. For some time he watched Thérèse carefully, though less for something in her than in himself. Could his vision, his subsequent angel-thirst, be a sublimation of a much more physical desire? And of what kind? Was it the girl he truly wanted, or perhaps — as he had never felt before; as he had often, to his barren wife, quite truthfully denied — a desire for a child of his own? But no. Thérèse was a beautiful child — even bewitching — but he was not bewitched. He could watch her with almost total equanimity, thinking only of angels.

15

Brussels, 16/ix/48

... And then you ask what I think is important, and as quickly retreat from it. You see, little has changed since you first wrote to complain that I did not answer your letters properly, truthfully, memory of which has surely had something to do with my several long silences since. I have to stop, and wait until I catch up with myself, until I come upon myself, like a mood, the mood of which you approve. Perhaps, I sometimes think, you only ask me such questions to make this happen. (What is the 'truth'?

How do I recognise it? Whenever I think I have found my 'real', my 'actual' self, I look behind it, I question it, and there is another one there!)

The answers, anyway, are at once extremely simple and, I suppose, complex. I have to do what I can for Angelique and Robert — to survive for them as long as possible, and I have to keep faith with Denise, though I must also not lose myself in either of these directions; I must watch that the trace elements are not all leached away. And I must work, because whether or not there is something original in what I compose, or in the places my mind must go or be taken in order that I may do so, my faith is there; it is all there is.

And (fourthly? and should I begin this 'But ....'?) there is also, since it is where the music is, where it comes from — a broader sort of affection, an emotional openness, an awareness that has to be maintained, that has to be striven for, even though there is so much working against such things that their most immediate reward is psychic or emotional damage. There is a level upon which people are so unused to being touched, to being noticed, that although their first response might be excitement, love, further openness, their second, close on its heels, is likely to be resentment, shame, even hatred. He or she who chooses to persist in such openness has to take upon themselves these things, the resentment, the shame, the hatred of others, and even (perhaps most) of themselves, again and again. I don't know why I feel that this, perhaps more than anything, has to be done (or perhaps I do know), but it does. Nothing lives, nothing means without it.

So survival, then, and keeping faith, and work, and continuing to feel, to be wounded rather than to wound. Although wounding is also a part of it, maybe inevitable. As you know.

This letter is a wound? Perhaps not, though it would wound.

And together — apart — we two are perhaps a wound (a tear?) in something larger. I do not pretend that any of this is easy.

12/iii/49

... Recently, at a reception at the Academy for a visiting conductor, I met Felix Murgati, a distant relative of Bernhausen. Indeed, it was to meet him that I went to the reception in the first place, since I had come across references to him in biographies. I was delighted to receive an invitation to his chateau to inspect some of B's papers that had come down to him through his mother. It transpires that he had in fact hoped I would catalogue them for him (there are almost two trunks of them), and that he himself had come to the reception in order to meet me! I now, in any case, find myself saddled with the work. It is not difficult and does not greatly interrupt my own. There is no time limit, and on the two visits I have made so far I have been amply repaid with the meals, the wines, Murgati's company, and the opportunity to bring Denise and the children to the chateau and its rambling gardens.

I would not mention this, but for the fact that at one point, taken into his spacious bedroom to see a large antique desk that had once been B's, I was stunned to find, on the wall, a portrait of a woman so like you that for some time I'm afraid I almost forgot myself. I passed it off, I think (for a moment I believe I actually went quite blank), but on the one occasion I have been there since I found myself listless, unable to concentrate, and had to struggle to put out of my mind the absurd desire to return to the room upstairs.

The painting is extraordinary. The eyes, in particular, burn. It was by someone in the school of Courbet. 'The unknown artist's unknown mistress', Murgati put it. It seems he bought the portrait over twenty years ago. He told me he had gone back to the gallery over and over again unable to imagine how he could pay for the piece, and yet unable to imagine living without it. How could I tell him that I knew exactly and more than what he meant?

1/vi/49

... a vain windbag. On at least one visit — it is not easy for me to find the time away from the orchestra, let alone, having found it, to resist taking it for my own work — he kept me talking (listening!) from the moment I stepped from the car, and ensured that no progress was made whatsoever. But I have almost finished the first trunk, and cannot say that it hasn't been worth the time and frustration. There are the manuscripts of several published works, the symphony among them, and in working through them I have found a number of variations and proof enough that, as I have long suspected, the versions we have been playing are not nearly those he might have dreamt of or originally intended. Most significantly I have found two short compositions no one has mentioned and which I am almost certain have been quite unknown before this, indeed have never been, could never have been performed. And such things! coming in each case, as if this were their point (in one of them it is twice, in the other it is actually three times), to a bizarre disharmony that works, though it should not, like a mathematical or a philosophical paradox. At first I wasn't sure that they were complete, but I now think that they are, that each composition is whole, but a whole made up of apparently (but I think only apparently) incomplete gestures. They are hauntingly musical, but as if in defiance of music. They seem, in fact, to have been composed as much to read as to play, since so much of their music is of the eye, the inner ear, in fulfilment of the very possibilities the piece as it would have to be played must perforce deny. A sort of suggested, technically implausible, physically inaudible music ...

27/xi/49

You present the problem so clearly, and I have made such a cloud, a miasma about it. I am sorry. Again, I am sorry. But it is not clear; at least the answer is not. I was disturbed again to read the term 'guilt', but will say nothing further until you tell me what you mean. Only this, that such emotions may not evaporate the more we ask Why, but they do become more essential, their roots more exposed. Most of these feelings are not really our own, or are far less so than we have been taught to believe. But if the individual will feel them, will take them upon themselves, then they take the onus from the collective. And that should not be. You are guiltless, blameless. If you feel that I am also, then that is one thing we may have learnt; that may be a part of the difference, and our 'disease' as you call it not a disease after all, but a key, an advantage, a kind of hidden strength ...

But perhaps that is not what you meant by your guilt, or your lover's fear. It seems, in any case, that it is very likely more or other than the act itself that scares him — some combination of moral wildness and moral rigour, if I have to put words to it: your eyes, that will not close, even in orgasm. At least, that might not, not then, not yet. Perhaps he is afraid that he won't be able to keep his own eyes open, that he may not be able to see, to breathe — to think 'clearly' — in the place you'd take him. Yet one can learn to love diving into such dark waters; even to need it. And the 'sexuality' may be only a symptom. It is unpredictable, volatile; it follows the laws of the body, not of the society. Probably that is why, in all of its 'normal', acceptable forms, it is so contained, within the night, the bed, the marriage. If sexuality could remain just that it would be the less disturbing, but when it moves outside the bed and the night (and, yes, the marriage) it seems to suggest — to threaten? — that other things in a person have also moved outside their normal restraints, that more than the sexual may be at risk. Hence the strange paradox that many men experience (but is it only men?): that, side-by-side with the sudden sexual intensity and excitement of a new lover, a new affair, is a kind of threat to the rest of their being ...

7/iv/50

... My work on B proceeds intriguingly. No more unknown compositions, but I have discovered lately in the second of M's trunks a journal almost as fascinating and that, again, it seems no one had known existed; a daybook, as B has titled it, though the opposite might be a better term. It is a collection of random jottings, ideas, sketches, drafts of letters, notes on books that he is reading, frequently interspersed with phrases, musical gestures these things may have suggested to him. It is of course full of gaps, and not even the shortest things really cohere, but it has ensnared me none the less — has a power, a character somehow beyond itself.

The other night, standing at the window, I realised how I felt about it. The stars for me seemed suddenly to serve only to indicate the vastness of the sky, of the darkness beyond and between and about them. The fragments in this nightbook do the same. Here there is a sentence, a scrap of an idea, like a tiny, isolated point of light; there there are a few sentences, almost a paragraph, like a sketch of something larger, a tiny constellation: but the gaps between the thoughts are as important as the thoughts themselves. Soon, in fact, they become essential, a virtual guarantee of the things, the fragments they separate. He wrote once of a desire to create something — a piece of music, a book — that would lay himself utterly bare, and claimed to have embarked upon it, but so far no one has been able to satisfy themselves that any of the things we have found of his could truly represent such an attempt. I do not imagine that this is it either, but it is the closest thing we have to it. Perhaps, in any case, he had never meant at all the kind of confession that some have thought he meant. Perhaps he was talking of a different nakedness. And perhaps, when we lay ourselves bare, we cannot cohere.

I have always wanted myself to write such a thing. Or rather, the want began to grow in me, was first planted when I heard of it. To hold nothing back. To tell, to put into words so that I myself have to see it, so that it is woven into the current of my life, how I sit up some nights, naked, unable to stop myself thinking of you, and masturbate, there, in the dark, although I am not alone, although Denise is sleeping in the next room. And then get up, and go back to bed, some of my own seed still clinging to my hands, feeling exactly what I am, a pathetic, wretched thing racked by an emotion I would call love or desire, but which is probably something else, immensity, exerting its direct pressure on the organism.

Sometimes it seems the only dignity left is in saying this, in saying Yes, I know this. This is what I am.

('To hold nothing back'! Isn't that what the stars do? The dark, the nothing behind them, held back by them, and yet made so much the more evident because they are there?)

16

In his second-floor bedroom, overlooking the moonlit courtyard, the Professor, uncomfortable in the midsummer night's heat, is dreaming that he is a large white cat in a dark cellar infested with rats. There are not a great many of them, but they attack him constantly, without fear, taking away small pieces of his fur and flesh in their needle-sharp teeth. He is shrieking, or trying to shriek, but no sound is coming out. The steps that used to lead up from the cellar have rotted, and though he leaps to what seem supernatural heights he can never reach the door. His paws are torn and bloody from the stone. The small squeals of the rats drill at his ears. He must leap and leap at the small square of light, but, strong as he is, the rats will soon tire him. Soon they will have stripped his pink flesh of its long white fur; eventually they will tear at his entrails.

Dawn with its grub-coloured edges drags him awake. Soon, as he hoped it would, the pungent aroma of strong coffee cuts through the anger's ragged outskirts, or starts to, though as he stands at the ground-floor window watching the first sun over Miklus' gables there is at least one violent backbite. But no, it is only the usual mad cock, who does not know when to stop. After the third crow there is the fourth, the fifth, etcetera.

The dream is not confined to the night. Sometimes it stabs at him even through the glorious tapestries of Wagner, the ordered autumnal forests of Mozart. Each day he must leap several times. They have almost exhausted him. Staring into the mirror he notes that as, ignoring the doctor, he sinks further and further into alcohol, his skin is becoming paler, his thin brown hair gradually turning snow white.

17

The writer, Bernard, lives at the rear of the building, in rooms that face northward. Outside their generous modern windows (installed only recently), the wide grounds, between high stone walls, descend in stepped gardens toward the river, beyond which, after a few straggling streets, can be seen open fields, a wood and, on a hillside in the distance, the beginnings of an extensive, new vineyard.

Not yet ready again for anything larger — having only recently completed a work of some substance — Bernard has returned to an ever-expanding collection of small pieces he calls 'studies'. These come unpredictably and inconclusively from the world about him — most of them from the house itself — and follow no particular sequence. He imagines indeed that anyone who cared to read them might arrange them much as they wished, shuffle them like a pack of cards perhaps, and set them out according to their mood.

At present, intrigued by ideas he has come across in a biography of Courbet (he is addicted, Bernard, to the biographies and autobiographies of artists), he is trying to write still lifes. It's a paradoxical task — sometimes, he thinks, a ridiculous one — yet he persists, fascinated by the difficulties and revelations it entails. On the windowsill in his kitchen, sharply defined against the sky beyond, are a brown stoneware coffeepot, a similar, corked jar in which he keeps the unground beans, a small wooden grinder with a corroded brass handle, an oil-flask and three brown bowls. They have been there for some years now, in one configuration or another, shifted about as are most such things in daily use, but as a still life they have only just now come to his attention — leapt into it, as if into sudden sharp focus, in that brief state of almost painful sensitivity which for him marks so often the onset of creativity.

He suspects that it is a losing battle. A painter, he reflects, most certainly begins his picture somewhere — with a sketch, a preparation of the canvas, some light-coloured wash — and builds upon it layer by layer, the detail eventually filled in, the canvas ripened through a thousand finishing touches, but in the end only the most experienced can see where the work might have begun. To others, the painting and all its features appear to exist in the one moment, the one plane of time, whereas he, the writer, is condemned always to be seen to work *in* or *through* time. If he began with a description of the coffeepot and moved gradually toward the oil-flask or the little pagoda of bowls, the reader would always move in this way with him: the flask would always follow the coffeepot, the bowls always follow the flask, the whole composition never at once seen whole, the first parts always already fading slightly as the last came into view.

As he wrote — as he added word to word, sentence to sentence — the very stillness of the image was sacrificed to a grammar which demanded verbs, subjects, predicates, commas, full stops where in fact there was only silence, coexistence, the one variegated and infinitely subtle noun. As if action, relation, were the price of verbal existence. As if an image, to become a thing of words, must take on order, hierarchy, even intrigue.

Sometime, perhaps, having achieved what compromise was possible, having worked out the necessary subterfuge, he will begin to write about people in this way: but the noun of a young girl, a young boy, an old woman — Mara Pizac, Michael Bloch, Mme Lecault — how could he write that?

18

How do you convince a ghost, who must very likely think that it is you who are the ghost, that you are real, and alive, let alone from another century? In all likelihood these, or some such things, might have been a problem for either of them, though as it happened it was Mme Lecault who first undertook the task, beginning carefully, gently, saying at first only that she had been sitting there, some time ago, and had begun to hear, and then to see the woman. The rest could follow later. It worked. Something about each other reassured them both, and within an hour, despite the years that separated them, and after one or two fine points of difference — Mme Berry would not accept, for example, that *she* was a ghost, not being dead, and took advantage of this brief conversational momentum to point out that Mme Lecault's status was even more questionable, it being impossible, she would have thought, to have a ghost of one not yet born — the two were almost like old friends.

It was not, after all, so difficult to establish what had happened. The old form of the house, it seemed, had continued to exist within the new — at least 'continued' was the term Mme Lecault found herself using, although to Mme Berry it was as if she, in 1769, were being visited by the future, or that their times were running parallel. She was also an insomniac, she told Mme Lecault, and shared the problem with her employer, an elderly General who passed the dark hours upstairs, on the other side of the house, writing his memoirs, although to Mme Berry this seemed more a matter of brandy and mumbling and staring at walls and windows than of pen, ink and paper. She was reluctant to speak a great deal more about her times and circumstance, although less out of superstition than out of some doubt for her own authority, spending as she did so much time more or less alone on the estate, and so many of her waking hours in darkness. She went into the town only rarely, she said, — it took just under an hour to walk there — and never had seen any other town but it. Little by little Mme Lecault began to understand from such things that the town in Mme Berry's time did not extend to the house — that the house in this time was part farm, part country retreat, the building itself shaped differently, the courtyard as she knew it not courtyard but open-ended, with a stable where now was Auguste's vegetable garden, and with an orchard, a hedge and then open fields where now were rue Beauclair and all of the streets to the river.

19

Part of the attic ceiling has fallen in the Bloch apartment. Not a hole exactly, but the plaster has been dislodged and one can see a board or boards behind it. Mme Bloch is inclined to think that it's the weight of the doves' nests — they have been roosting up there for years — but M. Bloch fears that there may be something wrong with the roof itself. There's no sign of a leak, at least not yet, but it may be that a tile has broken or fallen in. There is no telling how old the roof in that part of the house is. M. Bloch thinks that underneath the soot and lichen and pigeon dung the tiles may be eighteenth century. It may be a can of worms, he says, but someone is going to have to open it.

It's hard to get up there to see. The Professor, helping Mme Lecault out at a difficult time, got a man in to fix Valle's ceiling where the heavy light-fitting had been wrenched away, and he may well still have the name. Not a roof specialist exactly, but good anyway, and much cheaper. Perhaps, Mme Lecault thinks, it is time someone came; she might be able to kill two birds with one stone. A few weeks ago Thérèse and Stéphane Christophe heard an invisible cat mewing on their landing, and Alain had eventually found it and four newborn kittens in the space beneath the floorboards. One of the boards had broken as he took it up, and although a rug might cover it for the time being, in the long run it would have to be replaced.

The house is a bit like a body, Mme Lecault sometimes thinks, the flesh always changing over the bones, always something breaking, always something to be patched up. Scars. Sensitive places. Old wiring like varicose veins. A mind of its own.

20

Auguste has only one eye. No one knows where the other is, and Auguste himself isn't telling. Michael's first memory of him is of when his father took him out into the yard to see the gardener about something. The gardener was Auguste. Michael must have been about three years old and was toddling independently behind. On the way he had seen something on the gravel — he now thinks red grease perhaps, or jam, or even a rotting plum, which he had stuck his finger in and almost tasted before his father had plucked him away. At the end of the path was the garden shed and the chicken-coop, a chopping block with an axe in it, feathers. And then Auguste had come to the door, and he was not wearing his eye-patch, and there had been the pulsing red of the empty socket raw and bright and glistening wetly as if it had just been done, as if the eye had just been pulled out. Michael had thought immediately of the thing on the path and begun to scream. His father had had to carry him, his face hidden in his shoulder, all the way back to the house. For a long time after this the garden had been a place of terror. Nor had Auguste improved the situation when, coming home drunk and depressed early one evening, he had come across Michael playing in the courtyard — it cannot have been a year later — and leaning over him had growled and lifted up his patch, then staggered off rasping with laughter. His father had been angry. He had spoken loudly to Auguste. He had even spoken to Mme Lecault.

Eventually — since at heart Auguste was a gentle man, and had tried a gift of radishes, carrots and an apple the next time — things had improved. From a place of horrors the garden became a place of possible pleasures, and the demon at its centre something different. Michael had been given the run of the paths, to ride his tricycle about, then eventually of the fallow beds, to load and unload his big metal tip-truck, or build elaborate earthen fortresses, or racing-circuits for his miniature cars. By the time he was six years old he and Auguste had become firm friends.

It was at that age and on one of these visits when, looking for a place to hide his highwaymen before he brought the coach through, Michael saw a swarm of tiny black insects on a tomato plant and went to tell Auguste. As usual, he and the old man had been alone in the garden, at opposite ends, but now he found the place deserted and remembered that some time before Auguste had gone down toward the shed. Michael went down there and, finding the door slightly ajar, entered without knocking. The shed is a dark, earth-smelling place, cluttered with terracotta pots, rakes, hoes, mattock, axe, trowels, and a set of delapidated wooden shelves — only planks, really, separated by half-bricks and broken paving stones — covered with half-empty paint-pots and jars of rusty nails and hinges and screws. At the far end, by the window, are a table and chair where Auguste sits on wet days to drink coffee and read the paper, and sometimes falls asleep. He was sitting there now, with his back toward the door, and did not seem to notice that Michael had come in. The boy approached him quietly, thinking that Auguste might be dozing. Instead he was looking at a large magazine, with pictures of beautiful ladies that looked like flowers. Auguste looked at Michael with an expression that was both surprised and sad. When Michael asked him about the pictures he said that they were of angels. He let

Michael look at them. They were beautiful, like the irises and roses and snapdragons Auguste had sometimes taken him to see. Someone at the printers had coloured them, the gardener told him. Some of them have red hearts, he said, and some pink, and the petals, too, come in different colours — white, pink, yellow, even a deep blue-black, with fine hairs about them, of yellow, or brown, or black, or red. Together they looked at them for a long time. Eventually, his attention having drifted to the dust-motes in the windowlight, the buzzing of a fly against the pane, Michael went out. It was late afternoon and the sun was bright and yellow on the lawns. The gardens, where the sprinklers had been playing on them, were giving off the strong, confusing scents of flowers.

21

An egg. A large cup of delicate, fragrant tea, and an egg. That, and a piece of thick, golden toast, still hot, a last disk of butter unmelted, testifying to the fullness of the rest. She towels herself dry, and lingers over dressing. It occurs to her that with Michael already at school, Jean-Luc at his office, M. Leotard away unexpectedly for a two-day hearing on the coast, this morning is a gift, anonymous and unreturnable, that would only be wasted alone in the lawyer's offices, and should be treated with the appropriate freedom.

Much of it is in the timing — a few seconds late and the tea is already too strong, the edge gone, the toast has cooled too much for the butter; a few seconds too soon and the white is too soft — and yet one cannot think about that, but do it as easily as a much-practised dance-step, breaking the egg into the skillet, into just enough butter, turning off the gas beneath it just after one has slipped the bread under the grill and turned up that, pouring the water into the pot immediately before setting the table with its white napkin, its white plate, the simple knife and fork, the large, wide teacup with the millefleur pattern, the thin slice of lemon on the saucer, using as a benchmark the brief moment of balance between the firmness of white and softness of yolk, the curtains already open, sash raised high on the summer air, light breaking clean and crisp and white across the kitchen, and then, buttering the toast, the benchmark reached, slipping the egg from the skillet, sprinkling the pepper, pouring the tea, sitting, leaning slightly forward to add the lemon before pausing, knife and fork raised, to draw a deep breath full at once — if one thought about it, and the joy is that one doesn't — of childhood and maturity, freedom and control, solitude and plenitude and vacancy, knowing that the taste is yet to come, the moment when the knife cuts the membrane of the tiny sun and the yolk-light spills over the toast and the white, when the hot fluid rinses the mouth of the first bite, makes way for the next, the flavours of egg and tea, pepper and sunlight and memory mingling, knowing that this need not be all, that this is simple, that it has just been done, and can be done, again and again.

22

For several days after the incident in her father's apartment, Michael is too shy to seek out Thérèse, afraid that she had really been awake, that she had been too horrified to speak, but when she herself comes to find him nothing seems to have changed. She makes no reference at all to that afternoon, and he assumes with relief that she had truly been sleeping, that she knows nothing of what he had done.

Scarcely a week later, however, on a similar warm and empty afternoon, he goes to see her, as they have arranged, but receives no answer to his knock. The door is unlatched. Sure that she will be somewhere at home, perhaps just out of earshot, but also afraid to call out lest he wake her father who is sometimes at home and sleeping at this hour, he pushes the door open and enters.

The apartment is on the upper floor, facing the courtyard. He finds her seated in an armchair in a corner of the dining room, sashed by a wide shaft of sunlight. Her arms are thrown back and her hands clasped behind her head. Her left leg is raised on a high footstool. She seems again to be asleep. The cat is on the floor before her lapping at a saucer of cream. Thérèse is wearing red slippers and a red skirt that, in order to sun her legs, she has drawn far back to reveal a fresh white petticoat and a glimpse of white underwear. Michael stands by the window and watches her for several seconds. Eventually, as if she can control it no longer, but with her eyes still closed, she breaks into a broad smile.

23

The house is overrun by cats. Not only are there always three or four in the courtyard and as many evident on the roof, but there seem to be one or two in every apartment — or would be, if Mme Barber, M. Bloch and Mme Pizac worked any less hard at keeping them out. Indeed, with these few exceptions, a willingness to live with cats is a virtual condition of occupancy. Cats witness almost everything that happens here, their hard, wise faces suggesting that there is little that could surprise them, that they have seen everything before, that there is a good deal that they might tell, if someone were to court them sufficiently. And perhaps this is true. Cats like to be with people; they warm when two or more humans are together in a room. People, in heightened states of sensuality, approach the condition of languid cats.

The children have grown up with them. They have watched them fighting. They have heard them copulating on gutters and fences. They have heard their low moans, their loud, almost human wailing, their sudden explosions and scutterings. They have stared back at them when they were gazing like sphinxes. Most of all, they have watched them sleeping, yawning, lying outstretched with their soft bellies exposed, their eyes barely open. They have held them, stroked them, made them purr, have kicked them, hit them, fed them, been scratched by them, licked by them; they have slept with them sleeping on their beds. In return, it might be, they have learnt secrets of cats — and of things that cats know the secrets of — that they can tell no one but themselves, that they are probably unaware of learning and will very likely have forgotten by the time they are no longer children.

If it is true that cats have nine lives and that, as Auguste claims, the oldest cat in the house is nearly twenty, then it may be there are some cats here who have seen several human generations, and there is no telling, given their Egyptian eyes, how far their memory extends. Sometimes, looking at Thérèse or Stéphane Christophe, at Michael Bloch or Catherine Barber, at Tad or Mara Pizac, it can become quite suddenly apparent that it is cats' eyes that the house's children have, that it is as cats they sometimes stare at one, that there is every possibility that, like cats, their memories, their knowledge, the secrets that they know, stretch back for generations — that, as sometimes with a cat, one can find oneself looking into their eyes as over an inestimable distance, and that, if one were to reach out to them, to touch them, words would be found totally inadequate. That all they wished from one, in their strange, different indifference, would be that one stroke them, as one might a cat, and not otherwise invade their silence.

24

There are not many who are able to walk through walls with confidence. Mme Lecault had been none the less working on it, with and without Mme Berry's assistance. She was eager to know about the rest of the house — not her own, of course, but the older one, before it had been rearranged — and thought that somehow it might just be possible that she could be taken to see it. For a long time her hints appeared to fall on deaf ears: Mme Berry would either seem not to hear or would turn them aside with some gracious yet incontestable gesture, and change the subject. On the three or four occasions when, frustrated, Mme Lecault asked more directly, the conversation became a little stiff, as if she had committed an indiscretion, and at least once Mme Berry sought an early excuse to bring the meeting to an end.

This did not prevent Mme Lecault from trying in her own way. Perhaps, she thought, the walls became somehow soft at the times Mme Berry came and went through them, and on four or five occasions, as she waited for her friend to appear, or just after she had left, she pressed against the wall at the appropriate place, as if she fully expected it to give way. It never did. Clearly there was one wall for her own time and quite another for Mme Berry's.

She was not entirely discouraged. It might have been that actual contact was the key — that, if she could manage to hold on to Mme Berry's hand as she departed, then she herself, so deviously introduced, might also pass through. But to test this would require considerable patience. Mme Berry was shy of any kind of physical exchange. She would rarely, for example, accept so much as a cup of tea, and one time when Mme Lecault was so glad to see her that she had proffered to kiss her cheek, Mme Berry had good humouredly but firmly stepped away. Indeed discretion, reticence of this kind, became an unspoken law between them, keen enough as Mme Lecault may have been to break it. Mme Berry, after all, was no real ghost — at least, not of the insubstantial kind. She seemed, in fact, to take on more substance the longer she stayed, as if the immediate surroundings of the new, modern world in which she found herself depended somehow upon her confidence and concentration. The more she accepted Mme Lecault, for example, the more it seemed that the things about that lady existed for her also — so much so that on one occasion, as she turned in mid-sentence, her long, full skirts had knocked over the coffee table, and she herself had bent to set it to rights.

Conversation, ultimately, seemed the safest, likeliest strategy. If Mme Lecault couldn't touch, couldn't hold her way in, she would have to resort to talking it. Again this had to be oblique. Mme Berry, once she had begun, was often very happy to talk long and intimately, but was still reluctant to reveal very directly any physical details of her own domain. At one point, true, she had quite spontaneously picked up a pencil and started to sketch a kind of floor plan, but she did so only very crudely, and gave up before it was finished or she had filled in any detail, as if something had suddenly crossed her mind, and she had thought better of what she was doing — a fear of invasion, perhaps, or some subtler possession, that she might find no less irreversible.

Mme Lecault, however, could not understand why. She herself was keen to tell her friend whatever details of her life and times she expressed even the most tentative wish to know. Indeed it rapidly came to seem to her that Mme Berry was all but god-sent: someone with whom at last she might share the burden of the things that kept her up at night; someone to whom she could tell those secrets she had come to know that she could utter to no one else. Though such an openness might take time, of course, and it would be better for the moment to keep to less troublesome details — of how the house was now divided, say, or of who now lived where. She would speak, for example, with some pride of how the house had attracted artists, musicians, intellectuals; of how even now she counted amongst its tenants a retired professor, a countess, and a writer of renown. Indeed so mild and moonlit a night it was upon which she found herself speaking warmly of these things that she urged her friend to venture outside, so that she might point out their windows, the current shape of the house. But Mme Berry would not. Each, it seemed, had their own superstitions, their own way of handling the situation.

25

Just after first light, earliest dawn. The blue wash of the night has not yet left the courtyard or even the high gables, though, as Lucien watches, a pigeon rising from the apex of the roof turns briefly white before settling again as if upon an invisible ripple of air. Wakened by something now untraceable, and knowing from long experience that he will not go back to sleep, he has just opened the door of his children's bedroom. A ripple seems to pass through them also. Stéphane stirs and sighs deeply; Thérèse, almost before her brother's movement finishes, breathes sharply in and rolls toward the light, as if the dream of each were responding in its own fashion to the gentle shifting of air from the opening door, or their father's own gentle moment of inspection. The curtain at the half-opened window then billowing silently, and a pulse coming and going in his chest, as if life itself also, waking or sleeping, might sometimes respond to a similar stimulus, a similar movement or moment of inspection.

26

Although he has seen the Professor about the house for as long as he can remember — glimpsed him almost daily coming or going from the library, the markets, the Café de l'Odéon, or in the side lane taking out his garbage, or sitting at his window, as he does so often during the summer evenings, watching the courtyard with the classical music filtering out — and although the old man has sometimes nodded to him or smiled, Michael has never actually spoken to him. But now Mme Lecault wants the address of a workman that she thinks the Professor has, to give to M. Rocquart who will be here soon, and she cannot leave the jam — the smell of the plums was even down at the street corner when Michael was coming home from school.

He knocks with some trepidation, and after a few moments, the door not opening, thinks he might be spared. But it is not to be. Just as he is about to back away, having knocked, not too loudly, a second time, he hears shufflings and a muffled voice, then the rattle of a doorchain. 'Dear boy,' the Professor says when he finally gets the door open, 'what brings me this pleasure? Why don't you come in?'

It is the last thing that Michael wants to do. The Professor is in his dressing-gown and his face is yellow against the darkness of the apartment. Perhaps the knocking had brought him down from his bed. Perhaps that explains the faintly sour smell. But no, this isn't the case. He always works in his dressing-gown in the morning, he says — it is one of the luxuries of being 'retired' — and today he has been so busy with one of his projects that he has quite forgotten to get out of it. But will Michael please come up to his study — somehow Michael has come over the threshold and the door has closed — since he has his 'black' feet again and doesn't want to have to go up and down more often than he needs to, or down and up, again, as this case would be?

Michael follows the Professor along a short, darkened corridor and up a narrow staircase like that in his own family's apartment, past a set of small, dense etchings in silver frames: an old man gesturing angrily from a mountaintop, long hair and beard flowing in the wind; another old man — it might be the same one, though here he is holding scrolls in his hand — shouting from the steps of a temple, the great doors standing open behind him; and, in a third, naked ladies lying about in a tangle of clouds, a wise-looking king on a throne pointing to angels in the sky. 'My Fuselis,' the Professor says, pausing and turning toward him, 'I'm sorry that it is too dark to see them properly, but the light globe has burnt out and I can't reach to replace it. Perhaps' — smiling at the messenger — 'you can ask Mme Lecault to arrange something'.

The study is lined with books untidily arranged on the shelves with folders and papers, boxes and ornaments and cardboard tubes filling all the available space about them. There is a thick, richly coloured rug on the floor, an old leather armchair and a sidetable littered with dirty plates and glasses, and a large desk beneath the window on the only clear, un-book-lined side of the room. It is covered with pencils, papers, open books and some small photographs in frames — one, Michael notices, of the Professor as a younger man in a dramatic posture in a play, and another, even younger, in a monk's habit, with a group of other men dressed similarly. In a space at the front of the desk, before the simple wooden chair with a knitted cushion tied into place on the seat by blue ribbons sewn to its corners, there are several sheets of writing paper, some of them covered in a small, neat hand, and a green fountain pen left lying loose, mid-sentence, in the middle of a page.

The Professor begins rifling through papers and envelopes in a wooden tray at the side of the desk. While he does so Michael's attention is caught by a large, framed print on the wall to the left of the window. It is a vast carnival of people and animals, or so it appears, in a landscape of green fields and blue waterways, with birds and fruit and fish as big as the people themselves, and the people all naked, one man — or is it two? — with an owl for a head, another sleeping in a mussel-shell, others crawling into the empty tail of a gigantic lobster or riding, in a green leaf, on the back of a camel.

'Do you like it?' the Professor asks. It is difficult to say; 'like' may not be the word. But Michael cannot hide his intrigue.

'It's *The Garden of Worldly Delights*, by Hieronymous Bosch — part of a set of three, a triptych, that are painted to go side-by-side. It's only a print, of course. I don't have the room to hang it all. The first is too pious anyway, and I don't like the third as much as I used to. I have them somewhere ...' The Professor has found, in any case, the address of the workman and is writing it down. Before Michael leaves he has made out, also, a man with a blossom for a helmet, gnawing at a giant strawberry, jet-black women with bright red cherries on their heads, a couple, in the midst of a lake, riding in a giant bubble, and a man in the top right-hand corner with angel's wings, flying high above it all, carrying a large red ball.

27

Sometimes, on the best days, Bernard finds that even before he sits at his desk — while he showers, dresses, prepares and eats a simple breakfast (fruit, a croissant, a brioche, or part of a baguette with camembert) — he has already begun thinking about the piece that he is working on, his mind floating freely, almost effortlessly about an idea or description or fragment of narrative while the water sprays over him, or while later his hands perform the automatic tasks of cutting bread, spreading butter or marmalade, pouring coffee. At this time, if his sleep has been refreshing, and if he is not distracted early by some interruption or small irritation, whole stretches of his story, whole schemas of his argument can lay themselves out before him, so that he can find himself trembling, almost frantic in his desire to sit down with pen and paper, to begin sketching them before their delicate shape is lost or his miraculous but fleeting fluency evaporates. But these are the best days, the days of his inspiration. On most others — reluctantly aware, at last, after so many years, that his creativity is not a matter of ritual — his habits are rather different. If nothing has come to him as he was waking, or while he showered or dressed, he is more likely to eschew a home breakfast and to go instead to the Odéon if he wants to see friends, or the tiny Café des Origines where he is seldom disturbed and can sit sometimes for an hour or more inside by the heater or at one of the outdoor tables under an ancient umbrella drinking strong black coffee and alternatively reading the newspaper and staring vacantly at the square, as if something in the walk of the people or the pigeons, the complexion of the weather, the day's editorial might set his mind off, or at least tell him what kind of day it might be.

After a morning's work, a brief interval for lunch, sometimes a little more writing in the early afternoon, he delivers what he has done to Mlle Lupin, who types for him. This involves a walk of several blocks, but it is part of his ritual. He then spends the latter part of the afternoon in those other tasks — banking, correspondence, shopping, meetings, visiting friends — which he finds necessary in some way or another to support his work. This is not to say that the writing does not continue, or that he does not pause often in the market, staring at nothing in particular, or stop in the street to make a note on a scrap of paper, or push aside a book or letter, caught by some further idea or way of saying that had not occurred to him before, some fragment of a scene that has suddenly found necessity and form.

It is, he sometimes feels, as if he lives in two parallel worlds, so that even as he goes about the most menial of tasks he is also in one of the landscapes of his current text, conversing at one and the same time with an actual friend, an actual shopkeeper, an actual bank clerk in the rue des Girondins, and one of his own no-less-actual characters — watching a person in the street who is paradoxically both totally outside his fiction and in the process of entering it.

Some evenings he will spend with friends or at some entertainment: a play, perhaps, or movie or concert. Others he will spend with his sister and her family on the far side of the town. Most, however, he spends reading or on one of the smaller writing projects from which the main works — the *Studies*, the *Essays on Innocence*, *The Book of the Duchess* — have been keeping him. Always, however, whether before he leaves the house or after his return, whether before he begins his reading or much later, just before retiring, there is in his pigeonhole outside Mme Lecault's the familiar manila envelope from Mlle Lupin with the six or seven pages of neatly typed manuscript. He prefers to correct this on the day that it was written, not only for the sense of continuity it gives him, or because the ideas and contexts are still fresh in his mind, but also because it has always seemed to him to sow seeds of the next day's text, ideas that will germinate overnight to be revealed, fresh and shining, by the morning's shower.

28

Mme Pizac has never been large, but it is at least ten years since anyone has called her slim. It is not that she eats too much. Indeed, at dinner with Ivan and the children she will hardly touch a thing, though she does have a taste for cold roast vegetables and the fat from steaks and pork chops when they can afford them. No. It is something else. Some days she feels and looks as if she might explode. Not only red-faced, but as if her head and veins and heart are full to bursting. And her heart, too, will turn over at moments of its own choosing, as if the beats are stepping on each others' heels. And if, anyway, she does, from the chop, eat up the fat that no one else will touch, or drink with copious amounts of sugar a tea stewed blacker than most people have ever seen, those things could hardly begin to account for the fact that whenever she weighs herself the results are always ludicrous, insulting, quite beyond comprehension, as if she were made of a substance no one else is prepared to acknowledge or recognise. Ivan, for instance: when she forces him to look, can only suggest that the machines are wrong, although when he weighs himself the results are normal enough. *Of course* the machines are wrong; that is the point; but not in any way a man would see.

Maurois, for example. He wrapped a thing around her arm and pumped it and listened through a stethoscope, frowning. He told her that she had to be calmer, to work less, to rest, to lose weight, but when she exploded, when she demanded to know how, when she dragged her dress up over her thighs and belly — nothing he hadn't seen too often already — and said where? *what* weight? where *is* it? he only turned red himself, and asked the nurse to help calm her, and gave her pills. Not a single answer; not even a clue. His scales, the official ones, telling the same lie, and probably the other thing too, connected to his ears by the black rubber tubes, making him deaf even while it was supposed to be telling him whatever it tells. She long ago became convinced not only that people don't know anything like what they pretend to, but also that, like the bathroom scales, most of the instruments of measurement are wrong. Like mirrors. When, to check the placement of rouge, the hem of a dress, she looks in the mirror — she doesn't like to do it, but you have to, if only to make sure you're not making a fool of yourself — she cannot find, beyond the redness of face, beyond the lines and wrinkles and creases the weight makes as it drags her down, any evidence, but then the mirrors lie no less than the rest of them. The person you find in the mirror is only the person you have come to inhabit: it is never yourself. The mirror only tells about surfaces, never anything about what is really happening, or why. The eyes. You only have to look at the eyes, to know that someone is trapped.

29

Unnoticed by almost everyone — except, perhaps, their small group of friends and Mme Lecault, who notices everything — Michael and Thérèse have formed an indissoluble unit. They spend most of every day together. Much of the time they read, play cards, listen to the radio or play the piano, just as their parents might imagine they do. Sometimes they play with Thérèse's brother Stéphane, or with her friend Katia. There are days, however, when they play special games, games neither invites anyone else to share. As if with an innate sense of proportion, these are unpredictable and infrequent. Often they begin unintentionally. When they occur, however, their limits are of the imagination only and their rules, where there are rules, wordlessly understood.

One day they are playing cards. Bored with the simple games they know, Thérèse tells Michael of a different game she has heard of, in which people take off their clothes, one item for every hand that they lose. They do not know how to play this game, but it is not hard to improvise. Michael loses a lot at first, but then, when he has only his underwear and shorts left, Thérèse begins to lose also. She has tiny breasts, with tiny dark-brown nipples almost identical to his own. And, like him, just a few short dark hairs beneath her underwear.

One day, another day, they are drawn to M. Christophe's liquor cabinet. It is not with the intention to drink, but because a strange, tiered decanter has caught Michael's eye, a glass decanter with seven spouts, each capped with a small gold top, and seven separate compartments each holding a different brightly-coloured liqueur. Some of these liqueurs are semi-transparent, some are creamy, two are as clear as water, and all have strange, exotic names — advocat, blue curacao, abricotine, prunelle, triple sec, liqueur d'or. 'Do you drink them?' Michael asks. 'Yes.' 'What do they taste like?' But she doesn't know. They have never been opened. Her father doesn't like such things. They were a gift from someone a long time ago, when her mother was alive: a joke, she thinks. 'Shall we try them?'

Together they decide that a small taste of each will not be noticed, and one by one they unscrew the caps, removing the tiny corks beneath them and putting their lips to each spout in turn. Strange, unpleasant at first, the different drinks all seem to have, after the first sweetness, a taste like oil or petrol. By the time they come to the fifth, however, the sweetness has taken on its own appeal. Replacing the decanter, tilting it so that she can fit it into the tight, dark space at the back of the cupboard, Thérèse spills on her wrist a little from a spout they did not properly reseal. It is one of the clear liquids, the one she liked the most, the one that tastes of oranges. Without thinking, she puts her wrist to her mouth and licks, and then, a tiny trickle left, offers her wrist to Michael and laughs with pleasure as he sucks it.

Taking up the decanter again, she trickles a little more on her arm, and offers it to him again, then, this too licked off, trickles a little on her leg. When the game finishes, half of the clear, magical liquid is gone. In fact — he with his shirt, she with her white blouse off — Michael and Thérèse have quite forgotten it, the taste of skin having supplanted the taste of oranges: the taste of warm, dry skin in late summer sunlight, with the scent of the warm persian rug, the warm polished furniture, the faint perfume of fruit, of soap, of flowers.

30

Strange things will sometimes happen to Lucien Christophe. It seems that there are moments when he slips into the past or future, though he cannot properly tell. Not the distant past or future, nor particularly unfamiliar, but certainly not as familiar as the present can be. Most often it is a simple thing that might have a ready explanation: a slight rearrangement of his books or furniture, or the return of something he had thought he had thrown away. But sometimes, rarely, it is more, as when he discovers a set of his dead wife's clothing, thrown on the bed in the way he remembers from the time in Poitiers — clothes he had been absolutely certain had been thrown out long ago — or when, some two or three years ago, sitting with Thérèse on his knee, he became aware that in some way it was also not Thérèse, that the absence of a small birthmark behind her right ear, the cut of her hair, something in the eyes, confirmed a Thérèse apart, a different Thérèse, a Thérèse slightly older, and that his own clothes, the trouser-legs beneath her, the waistcoat buttoned over his chest and belly, were clothes he had never seen before. Lately — that this has happened twice seems particularly perplexing — it has been finding, on his own pillow or in the bedclothes beside him, a long, black hair, a woman's, when, for a period so long now that it makes him ache to think about it, there has been no such woman with him, even in his dreams.

31

Thérèse is playing cards. It is not the usual pack this time, but the tarot. She is playing alone, laying out the cards in various patterns, trying to work out the story within them. She begins to think that they may be a clue to the secret of the house, for she is sure that the house has a secret, or many, that are all part of a larger one. For an hour or more, in the afternoon sunshine, the faint yellow scent of a roasting chicken pervading her consciousness, she tries to work out which of her neighbours matches which card. Who, for example, would be the Queen of Wands? Who would be the Hierophant? Who could be the beautiful lady in the eight of swords, bound and blindfolded in the marshes with the castle far behind her, the sharp swords standing hilt upward in the mud and the reeds about her?

Her father, she thinks, is the tall man in the five of cups, or else the sad king of pentacles, and Michael is the page. Tad Pizac, having just walked by with a scowl on his face, has fixed himself forever as the nine of wands — of which Michael's father, M. Bloch, with his pipe in one hand and his silver-topped cane in the other, could be the two.

32

'*Casus est talus*', thinks the Professor, sitting at stool, putting down his tattered paperback of *Thérèse Raquin* which he thinks some day soon he will have to use as toilet paper, 'that we spend one third of our lives sleeping, or at least in bed, chasing sleep, or rising from it. Six to eight hours per day. Let's say seven, though they say women need more. And then eating, preparing food, or even just buying, sitting at it. Two-and-a-half hours. Shitting, pissing, let's say twenty minutes a day — no, thirty, though for some that's a gross underestimate. And then washing, dressing, the time simply moving from As to Bs another hour at least. Shopping, cleaning, washing yourself......You could go on and on but it's exhausting, half of your life with shit up to your knees and elbows, and who writes about it? Nobody. Dante perhaps, his flatterers was it buried up to their necks in it. But nobody else. If it's like that for me what must it be for......Mme Pizac? A family's washing and cleaning and cooking, dirty nappies year in and year out hers and who knows who else's, sores and rashes and abrasions, mother and probably grandmother until death. The enormous tragedy in that woman's bent shoulders........ The stuff of fiction is not the stuff of life. Where is the Book of Insomnia, the Anatomy of Anxiousness, rolling around in twisted sheets, the mind's sickly midnight cud? Where is the Book of Sex? Banned, if ever it appeared, but for most it's the longest novel after the Book of Sleep. Certainly the most interesting. Coming back to it daily like it or not, yet if you wrote it what would they call you? Where is the Book of Shit? They must have been all of them like that, up to their .... knees or waists in it, Donizetti, Bruckner, Barber, Albinoni, Mozart, notes like .... or .... orchids from the compost heap; or Fauré with his requiem and his choir boys. The whole thing like a great bush of candle-flowers, work after work with its filamentous roots deep in the blind invisible, one in grey sudless water another in the urinal a hundred in uns . . . leepable night . . . . ' The business coming at last, all the crumbling warm wet stinking soup. The Professor then reaching for the real toilet paper, looking into the upper corners for the putti that are never there. Or are, but rarely if ever deign to make themselves visible. Then, flushing, turning his nose up at a sudden strong smell: his own, yes, but also something else, as if the cistern itself had just belched.

33

The house is haunted, but there is almost always a logical explanation. Pipes have been covered over, blocked, re-routed. They also rust or are in other ways eaten away, air, sound flowing where once water did. Not often, but sometimes, voices can begin where there were no voices before, connections occur that are quite inexplicable to those who might witness them. A brick falls in an invisible tunnel and a rat, suddenly trapped, bangs and bangs itself against the inside of a wall. Soot falls, or mortar, and a chimney that had long been blocked and forgotten becomes a pipe, a funnel through which suddenly the wind can whistle where it had never yet done so, or shouts, laughter, singing from one room begin to issue, muffled, into another two floors above or two apartments to the right. In this way people become heirs to things they cannot understand or use — voices that cannot properly be heard but that are still voices, sounds that cannot be identified but are still sounds — and, having no other avenue, call them by inappropriate names. It is as if the old house had a subconscious, or there were layers to its consciousness, and places — hidden openings, passages, miniature corridors — where one level connects with another.

It is not only the small spaces — the disused fireplaces, the redundant sewage pipes — that disappear or resurface, after long neglect, in different guises. In more than one apartment the attic has been sealed for decades, perhaps longer, and while the tenants would very likely assure one that they know that an attic is there, it may in truth have slipped from their own consciousnesses for nearly as long, or been thought about, if it ever was, only as a vague possibility, something to be investigated later. Who could now know, for example, that in the partitioning of 1893 there were at least two small rooms — maid's quarters — that, should anyone have attempted a kind of architectural auditing, would never have been accounted for? Who could know of the room walled in — its windows removed, even its shared chimney rerouted — by General de Renteuill? Who could know, too, of the cellar that in 1870, for fear of the Prussian invaders, was bricked up so carefully that none but the owner and the highly-paid mason could ever tell where the new wall started? The former died only weeks afterward, still waiting for the Prussians, and within a year the craftsman himself had moved to Paris, never knowing and so never able to tell that he had once immured some of the best of Laffitte, Latour, Mont Rachet, Haut-Brion, Branne-Mouton, Chambertin, La Perriére, Pichon-Longueville, and a good many other priceless vintages of the pre-phylloxera, their sole visitors, as they nursed their own rich secrets in the darkness eleven feet beneath the courtyard, a few small spiders, a few tentacular roots of a lemon tree.

34

Again she tells him to take his clothes off, and again, likewise undressed, she straddles him, but this time it is in the living room, on the persian rug. Reaching over to the table, she takes down her set of paints, her brush, the cup of water, and, beginning broadly between the shoulder blades and tapering to tips almost two-thirds of the way to the elbows, begins to paint upon his back. The work takes the best part of an hour. Each feather, and there are dozens, is itself a wing, upon which are suggested further feathers that are also wings.

The work is so intricate, proceeds so slowly, that before she has finished the outline of the second wing, the first, because of the heat, because of the trickles of Michael's perspiration, because of the silent tears he knows nothing about, has begun to run, to blend invisibly into the deep, deep scarlet of the rug.

The Plank

1

THE Professor is again in his study and the music has begun, softly at first, but becoming louder as the afternoon wears on. Floating through the window it coats the stones like an invisible film of warm water. Sinking into them, entering the undersoil, the foundations, the cool darkness of the forgotten cellar, it also rises, spilling into other windows, pervading the courtyard rooms, entering unobtrusively all those who pass through them and also the children playing in the courtyard. It enters Mme Ségur who all afternoon has been trying for the first time to bake bread. It enters Mme Lecault as she stands by her kitchen sink lost in the immaculate dark-pink bulbs and long, delicate roots of the radishes she has just now taken from her shopping basket. It enters Stéphane Christophe, who is lying on the floor in his father's room engrossed in a story of Tintin. It enters the invisible and visible shadows. It enters the ants. It enters the green leaves and bright yellow globes of the lemon tree. It enters the cats on the wall watching the pigeons who, also entered and knowing it will soon be dusk, are just now rising and preparing to bank westward, over the apartments, to the high red roofs of the orphanage, three blocks away.

2

For quite some time now Axel Ségur has tried to disguise his obsession from Hélène, but eventually the proliferations of cherubim and seraphim can be explained away no more. It is simply that he feels better in such company than not: that, whether at home or in the office of his exclusive establishment, he likes — no, more than likes: needs — to have his latest small, winged acquisition within reach, to feel that its eyes might touch upon him if and when they would, or that he himself can look across whenever he wants and, by the half-closed lids, the unearthly innocence of the face, be calmed and reassured. At first a small corner of his premises was set aside for them, but this was quickly filled, and angels have begun to clutter the Empire chairs and chests and escritoires in which he otherwise specialises. Soon, in his large front window, the suit of armour that has for so long been his sign has been replaced by the tall weathered wings and frequently retouched blond curls of a large wooden figurehead from a seventeenth-century Dutch merchantman. Soon too the three or four small figurines he'd thought to house in the apartment have multiplied and their seraphic faces and cherubic hands, their nimbuses actual or intangible grace each and every room.

Hélène resists them. When four, five, six appear in the living room alone, when a second appears in the bathroom, a third in the kitchen, when a gilded plaster statuette replaces the vase of flowers in the hallway, she insists that Axel remove all but one or two of them to the spare room on the second floor, and that when this room is filled no more be brought into the house. It is not the overcrowding alone that troubles her, but the persistent suspicion that, if not actual madness or a sudden religious fervour (almost synonymous, in her thinking), their proliferation reflects somehow upon her own shortcoming, bespeaks a desire so long repressed that it has erupted in a bizarre, almost-aggressive compulsion.

It is none of these things — his own fears, after all, have been quite different — but understand or deny her suspicions as he might, Axel can not stop. He reduces his purchases and becomes more selective. He even regretfully sells certain pieces (not his finest) or returns them to the shops and galleries from which they came, but his fascination becomes only the more intense for his attempts to curb it. He marvels, even rails at it himself, but feels ultimately that it is not he that is the problem, that he has been chosen, is being *spoken*, and there is nothing he can do about it. As Hélène requests, he removes the bulk of his collection to the upstairs room and, when this becomes too crowded, changes his plan. Henceforth he will have to look not for more but for better angels, although for a time the definition of this 'betterness' perplexes him. The most ancient, expensive, ornate or beautiful alone will not suffice. After some confusion he begins to trust increasingly a kind of seventh sense to lead him to qualities he'd never suspected and would find difficult to articulate.

His business suffers accordingly. Angels are not as popular and lucrative as Empire escritoires. When, in a German auction catalogue, he finds one of his own first, unconscious angels, his

Bellinis, the memory of which has recently begun to haunt him, he finds that he has to sell, often at heartbreaking prices, by far the greatest part of his collection to meet the sum. This troubles him greatly at first, but eventually begins to seem a sign. Henceforth, with the Bellini now proudly in his possession, his acquisitions have to be even more cautious. Many pieces he might once have bought immediately he now eschews, preferring instead to take his instruction from dreams or some uncanny compulsion, some refinement of the seventh sense, which, though it visits him only rarely, can never be resisted when it does so. His collection is now far smaller and grows more gradually. Sometimes, though he might have afforded the more expensive, a tiny, handcarved children's angel-doll that might have cost a mere two or three francs takes precedence over a rare and exquisite example from the quattrocento. Sometimes, cued by the same ineffabilities, he chooses quite consciously the inferior of almost identical angels set before him. On at least one occasion, he goes a great deal out of his way to see a gallery he has no tangible reason to expect anything from, knowing that there will be a particular, unanswerable angel waiting for him.

3

A large brown envelope arrives for Michael. Mme Lecault tells him that the Professor put it in the Bloch pigeonhole on his way out in the morning, and that he had been looking for Michael the afternoon before. Inside are an oversized postcard of the painting in the Professor's study and two larger, coloured prints which the old man says in a note are the other panels of the triptych. One is called *The Earthly Paradise*, the other *Hell*. The note says that, much as the Professor would like to be able to give them to him, they are lent to him only. Would he bring them back when he has finished with them? Or leave them in his mailbox? There is no urgency. He is welcome to take his time.

Michael has drawn them part-way out of the envelope but with Mme Lecault watching he does no more than glance at them. Instead he takes them to his own room. Only there, with the door closed and his parents not home, can he look at them properly.

The Earthly Paradise surprises him. It doesn't seem like Paradise at all. God is in the garden with Adam and Eve, and Adam and Eve are both naked. He supposes that they look serene but there is also something else about them. Eve has her eyes downcast and Adam is looking at her with a kind of detached wonder, as if he does not properly see her or has simply never seen such a creature before, and God himself is staring out blankly toward the watcher. It is as if none of them is quite sure what they are doing there. Near Adam's hand a spotted cat is carrying off a rat (were there rats in Paradise?), and below it a bird is picking out the entrails of a frog. To the right and beneath the place where God is standing, a three-headed bird is shrieking at a group of strange creatures swimming in a pool so dark it might be oil: a miniature unicorn, a porpoise with a bird's head, a large fish with elaborate wings. Beyond them, behind the thick hedges, is an ornate pink fountain on an island in a shimmering blue lake at one shore of which a huge three-headed monitor is leading an exodus of frogs, turtles and smaller lizards. A giraffe, an elephant and a larger unicorn dot the distant fields, and seem peaceful enough, but there is also a lion devouring the carcase of a deer, and a large, whippet-like creature fleeing a wild boar.

Hell, on the other hand, seems far more what people claim it to be, although even here there are some puzzling contradictions. At the centre is a pair of thick, whitened stumps supporting a man's head and a body like a monstrous egg, through the cracked end of which can be seen a tavern in which naked drinkers sit. The stumps of this man-tree are not planted in the earth but supported by boats floating in a lake of breaking ice. Some people are trying to cross the lake on skates or sleds. Others have fallen through thin patches and are struggling in the black water. To the right of the man-tree, rising out of the lake, is a vessel of some sort — perhaps a copper vase — above which a great knife is precariously suspended. The knife in its turn supports a plate upon which a man in partial armour is having his bowels eaten by a pack of dogs. Below them someone is riding a naked woman into an overturned goblet and, further down, on the near shore of the lake, a blue-vested bird on a high throne is devouring people whole and excreting them, undigested, in transparent blue globes through a hole in the bottom of the throne into a dark pit into which other, smaller figures are also shitting and vomiting. Nearby a pig in a nun's habit is being taught to write and people at an overturned gaming-table are being ridden by demonic monkeys, or eaten by hounds, or stabbed by their fellow humans. There are also figures crucified on harps and lutes, or with flutes or brushes or awls screwed into their behinds. It's a nightmare party, a grotesque carnival. And yet, horrid as it is, there is pleasure in many of the faces; human figures cooperate with devils; not everyone is suffering.

The top of the picture is different. Here it is dark and more as Hell is supposed to be. There are walls and beacons of flame outlining dark masonry and the shapes of ruined buildings, a whole city burning. Hordes of naked people are being driven by mounted soldiers, and here and there a spar of light from a blazing tower or steeple exposes a great river of bodies. In places the river has become clogged or dammed, creating a terrible crush of flesh. People are clambering over one another. Others lie trampled in a tangle of limbs by the wayside. Details are hard to make out. The bodies are tiny. Clambering backward off his bed to fetch a magnifying glass, Michael finds his own joints aching and realises that, tense and rigid, he has been lying almost motionless for hours.

4

14/vii/55

Late at night, or very early in the morning. I woke and found that there was something I had to explain to you, or perhaps it was that I had to tell someone — tell you — something I had only just explained to myself.

Looking back over my life, it seems to me that I have always sought commitment in relationships with others, and have accepted it willingly. In fact I seem to have placed a great deal of emphasis upon it, to have given it a central position. I have also violated it, placed it over and again in jeopardy by beginning further relationships, usually sexual and usually clandestine, which the partner in the first relationship, the central relationship, would not tolerate if they knew. It comes about against my better judgement — of course! — and sometimes I think it is almost against my desire. This happened with Collette and with Jeanne, before I knew you, and because of you — of us — it has happened again with Denise. It seems to me that the most devastating thing that could ever occur in my life would be to lose that central relationship, and yet I place it in jeopardy. In the past I've explained this as a need for sexual excitement, for erotic adventure, having found over and again through my life that some part of the mind seems to flourish upon such things.

Now suddenly it occurs to me that it is not the eroticism alone. It is also the limitation, and a dimension of tension, of risk, of peril, which may be itself a further eroticism, an eroticism beyond or behind eroticism, and which eroticism itself only occasions — a means of breaking through, psychologically, creatively, to that place it has always seemed individual lovers break through when they climax, when momentarily they lose control of the self at one level and with a cry, a sob, a shudder, slip into some darker, wilder, totally unsocialised and exiled place. To make this place conscious, to look back from it is what I realise, suddenly, I have been striving for. And the essence of this place is risk, and the essence of risk is the paramountcy, the centrality of what is risked. It is also for that reason a place of terror. Sometimes I feel that to go there, to know more about it, I will have to lose everything, to throw myself in. And yet what am I, if I do not?

No, you will say, that is merely an excuse for exploitation, indulgence, sex-for-the-sake-of-something-else, without caring. But that is just it: the beauty of it, its bizarre, vile attraction, is that it cannot work, it will not work without caring.

Which is to say something else, to you, still.

5

Michael is again looking at one of the war books of Lucien Christophe, the frozen corpses of Russian soldiers killed in the battle of Suomassalmi, bewilderment on the face of a man in Amsterdam as he stares at the body of his young daughter lying in the street. He closes his eyes and they disappear; he takes his hands off the volume and it is as if it is no longer there. *Does all this exist only because I see and touch it? If all this is going on in my head, then what kind of head do I have? If part of me is seeing the flowers and the cat, then could it be that a part of me is also death? Where is that part when I am not looking at it? Does it go away?*

6

Mme Pizac — Marguerite, as she is called by those for whom she cleans or launders — has awoken with the uneasy suspicion that something is wrong. It is not quite six on an unusually cold morning in early autumn. Ivan is snoring — perhaps it is that which has woken her — but this at least is reassuring. She rises and puts on her dressing-gown, then moves to the window and lifts the curtain aside. The courtyard is still largely in darkness. Only a few dead leaves are moving over the paving stones. But the sheer emptiness itself is somehow comforting. At least it means that nothing so unusual has happened as to have people opening doors, moving about, turning early lights on in the cold.

Finding her slippers in the semi-darkness, she moves into the kitchen and lights a burner for the kettle, trying all the while, as she struggles to wake properly, to remember what she had been dreaming. Unable to recall anything, she begins to suspect that the feeling must have some other origin, though she cannot for the life of her think what it might be. Everything the day before, as she begins to go over it, had seemed quite normal, but there's always the chance that you have missed something, and she tends to believe her feelings: she could list a dozen times when they have been more reliable than the advice of someone who is supposed to know. Doctors, for example, though you can't tell. Maurois insists that there is nothing wrong, but what would he know? It isn't his body that he is talking about. It isn't his side, his belly. But the pain — that pain — has gone now. It isn't that.

Struck by a sudden thought, she moves off quickly to the children's bedroom. Tad lies in an awkward ball facing the wall, breathing heavily but steadily. Mara, behind the door — she has to go further in to see her — is lying flat on her back, arms flung out and a puzzled look on her face, as if somewhere in some other reality she has encountered a snag, but to all appearances in this one sleeping more or less peacefully. Moving carefully about the rest of the apartment — the light is stronger now — Marguerite tests all the windows and, finding most of them locked, checks on the few things of value she can think of. The money is still in the base of the clock on the mantel. Ivan's mother's silver, that arrived one day in a battered wooden box from his cousin, is still in the cupboard and her pearl necklace in the drawer. The radio is in the kitchen as it should be. Evidently it is not that either, and, when they wake, neither Ivan nor the children indicate anything that might help to explain. They are not used to having her ask such things, and she does not want to have to tell them. Not yet.

As the day progresses, however, the feeling does not go away. For much of the morning, as she cleans or darns or hangs out the washing on the lines at the back of the garden — there are not only her own things, but loads for Miklus, the Professor, the Christophes, and a large one for the Seracs on rue Thélin — she keeps an eye on the rest of the house and garden. Something might have happened to the Professor, for example, or Auguste, or Mme Bloch, who has not been well lately. But again nothing, nor when at almost twelve she goes to see Mme Lecault, knowing that she if anyone will know if anything out of the ordinary has happened in the house. Mme Lecault, in fact, has only good news, since one of her bouts of insomnia has come to an end and she has slept long and late, and woken refreshed, and the postman has brought her a card from her nephew the racing-car mechanic who is working in Italy. She always tells Marguerite about the mechanic, since Ivan might be interested to know.

There are other possibilities; one in particular. As the time grows closer, able at this point to think only of those most immediately around her — why should the feeling come so strongly, if it doesn't somehow involve her especially? — she becomes more and more convinced that this will explain things. As well as the washing she takes in, she cleans for various people in the house itself and in the neighbourhood. She does what she can with the apartments of Miklus and the Professor. She cleans also for Mme Maurois, the doctor's mother, who is now eighty-nine and very unsteady on her feet. It is her day today. Perhaps she has had a fall, or is ill, or has been taken to hospital. The sudden thought that she will find her dead, or hurt, and have to fetch people, has her almost frantic as she crosses the road toward the apartment — frantic, but then also a little relieved, since to know, even distressfully, is to put an end to the worry — but the bent-backed old lady greets her in the best of her sharp and sarcastic health, and nothing in her conversation, let alone the large, high-ceilinged, ornately-furnished rooms, gives her the slightest indication.

When she returns home she asks the children what has happened at school, but neither has anything unusual to tell. Nor does Ivan when he comes back from the garage. Indeed, to the contrary, he has been given a bottle of wine by a grateful customer, and seems only anxious to sit down to it with his fish soup and the fresh baguette. By this time the feeling has become a dull ache, scarcely perceptible when there are things to distract her, but stronger than ever when, the children back in bed and Ivan snoring again quietly in his chair, she sits by the window of the darkened living room, staring through a gap in the curtain at the empty and badly lit street outside, apprehensive, almost biting on panic, as if the cause might be in those hard-soled irregular footsteps she can hear approaching but, the walker being on this side of the street and the angle of vision so acute, can not see the cause of until they are almost upon her.

It is Miklus, of course, only Miklus, returning later than usual from his evening class at the Lycée. Tapping his cane in some obscure pattern as he walks, he sways slightly and hangs his head, as if he has been drinking.

7

The Countess makes love with her eyes wide open, watching every move. Her lovers rarely understand. They feel they are being judged, studied somehow, or worry that they should do the same. Never before have they realised how important it is to be able to hide one's face or to find, in the middle of an act of love, a mutual darkness in which to wander or suffer or come. Over and again they have asked her to explain, but she cannot. It is simply that her eyes do not or will not close. She cannot tell them — how could she? — that the grimace, the appearance of pain she witnesses has begun to fascinate her, the agony of the dying that they never otherwise admit they are. Nor can she tell them that it is not like this always: that there have been rare moments when the lids have fallen, as someone at the top of a precipice might close their eyes, or almost close them, and the eyes roll back, in the second before their legs give way.

The eyes of portraits also do not close. Is there some way in which the Countess may herself be a creation, a portrait of the woman that her lovers think she is? Perhaps this is closer to the truth of their discomfiture: to have this portrait, living, gazing back at one, as if this thing, this act, had never been seen before, as if one were doing something unusual, bizarre.

8

Do what Mme Lecault might to exclude it, the outside cannot always be kept at bay, even at those times she most hopes to avoid it. It is probably against just such intrusions that Mme Berry herself takes precaution in arriving so very late and so carefully. But precautions will not stop things from happening. The late-night sound of a motorcycle, shattering the silence as it clatters its way painfully over the cobblestones, the momentary cacophony of a garbage can upended by cats, even the noise of a last drunkard staggering along rue Thélin, are enough to have Mme Berry nervously on her feet, hands over her heart as if to prevent it leaping from her. And now, alarmingly, there is something more.

Mme Lecault and Mme Berry are sitting, as is now usual between them, by candlelight, and are so close in conversation that all thought of a world outside has long dissipated. Then suddenly, urgently, there is a knocking, not loud, but quick, sharp, alarming. Mme Berry pales instantly and, stiffening, seems about to flee through the wall. Motioning calm, her hostess rises and moves swiftly and silently into the darkness of the short passage.

The tiny window in the bolted door reveals the visitor's identity and allows Mme Lecault a moment's composure. It is, after all, only one of the tenants, also an insomniac, who once or twice, almost a year ago now, has borrowed a book to help them through the long night, although admittedly they have never before come as late as this. Clearly the soft glow of the candle is visible through the curtains, although what could have made anyone so bold or so desperate as to intrude at this hour is hardly apparent.

Her firmness rises even to this, however — her first priority, after all, is with the guest already there — and quickly, if very regretfully, before they have managed more than a handful of words, she has turned her unexpected visitor from the door, re-bolted it and made her way back toward the candlelit room, speaking quietly and she hopes almost off handedly in an attempt to calm Mme Berry:

'It was only one of the tenants, Madame, not normally so troublesome, but they are also insomniac I fear ... Madame? ... Madame?'

But it is as if Mme Berry had never been.

9

All morning Thérèse has been showing Michael her most secret possessions, her collections of treasures, her stamps and tiny pictures, her mother's things taken out one by one, each with its own story like the ghost-of-a-jewel, tiny and intricate and polished on the tongue. Even her favourite books, her favourite characters and scenes and sentences, opening one after another, leading him to them, reading them slowly and carefully, as if to share not only the sound but the taste of each as it passes from her mouth. And he has been responding with his own, finding her labyrinth so familiar that he himself can sometimes do the leading. Boxes lie strewn about them, open volumes, invisible creatures and people, and eventually an exhausted silence, languid and bemused.

Taking up her mother's cards, setting up the card table by the cluttered armchair, Thérèse begins to play patience, her favourite game, and soon is teaching Michael. He is tired now, and slow to pick it up. There is a second stalemate, then a third, and each soon becomes bored. It is as if the cards have minds of their own and are determined not to cooperate.

'Why are there only four suits?' he wonders, 'Why aren't there five, or six?'

'Yes, or eight or nine. Why are there suits at all?'

'Could you play like that?'

'Why not?' — he can see the idea excites her — 'And why not have our own suits, make our own picture-cards?' She wants to tell him that there are already cards like that, that she already has some, but something stops her. There are still some secrets she will not tell. 'There could be the Queen of Cats ...'

'Or the Prince of Frogs, and a Countess!'

'Yes, and a Professor.'

'What would we be?'

'We could be cats,' says Thérèse, abandoning the game entirely, gesturing, with the slightest flicker of a smile, to the shadows by the armchair where Gri, oblivious to the world about her, is cleaning herself meticulously: her paws, her face, her belly, her flanks, her anus. 'We could be the cats.'

10

May 1941. In Abyssinia an Italian army capitulates at Amba Alagi and the Duke of Aosta surrenders; on the 6th, Admiral Darlan and Herr Abetz, the German representative in France, sign an agreement for certain concessions in the occupation terms in exchange for German rights to use Syrian airfields; on the 11th Rudolf Hess, on a mission no one as yet fully understands, lands in Scotland in a Messerschmitt 110, and on the 20th the Germans, having taken possession of the whole of the Greek mainland, launch a massive airborne attack on Crete. At 6.37 a.m. on the morning of the 24th, in the freezing waters of the Denmark Strait between Iceland and the frozen Greenland coast the British warship *Hood*, engaging the *Bismarck*, receives a direct hit in the magazine and sinks, taking with her all but three of her crew. The *Bismarck* is chased for three days and over seventeen hundred miles before being sunk by the *Dorsetshire* about four hundred nautical miles west-south-west of Land's End.

There are photographs of the crew struggling in the black water, covered in oil. A few pages later, at 4 a.m. on the 22nd of June, Hitler launches his invasion of Russia. There is a large photograph of 'Nazi Hordes on the March'. Over the page there is a photograph of a young man squatting on a pavement beside a woman who is lying with her head on her arms. The young man is holding a tiny bundle. The caption says that he is a Russian father, and that he is holding his child while waiting for his exhausted wife to finish resting. It says that they are running away from the Huns. The man's face is partly covered, but it looks like M. Christophe. That is impossible, of course, but Michael imagines that that is who it is, and that he is holding Thérèse, and that the woman who is lying exhausted on the pavement — the woman who looks so much as if she is dead — is Thérèse's mother.

As he is flipping through the last pages of the volume — it is *The Second Year of the War in Pictures* — a newspaper clipping slips to the floor. 'Darlan Shot Dead in Algiers', it reads, 'Assassin Arrested'. A young man had shot Admiral Darlan when he returned to the palace. The young man was twenty years old. Admiral Darlan's chauffeur ran into the building when he heard the shots, and hit the young man in the jaw, but the young man made no attempt to defend himself. 'I surrender', he said, 'my revolver is empty.' It is also impossible, thinks Michael, that that young man could have been M. Christophe, or even his own father, although their ages would have been just about right. They would have shot him, the young man, he is almost certain of that.

11

In one of the upstairs rooms late at night a single lamp is burning, bathing all about it in rich, honeyed light. The room, although no larger than several others in the house, seems particularly spacious, almost cavernous, its long shadows reaching high towards the lofty ceiling and its ornate but unusable chandelier or stretching out across the open floor. It is sparsely furnished: apart from a small gas heater and one large threadbare rug spread out upon the polished boards there is only a bed, a large, sleek, iron-framed construction richly endowed with pillows, blankets, sheets and an eiderdown, though at this moment most of these have been thrust aside and there is, at the centre, as if castaways upon some warm, forgotten island, or drifting carelessly far out at sea, a pair of lovers.

For some hours now, oblivious to everything but the womb-like glow in which they flail, caress or languidly turn, they have been assuming the different shapes that are one of the vocabularies of lovers. Sometimes their shadows on the walls are like those of monstrous insects, sometimes like the ghosts of witches dancing about a blazing fire, although now, totally unaware of observation, they are too amazed, astonished by what is happening to them to notice any such things. Raw and sensitive from his caresses, her breasts, as she rocks above him, have begun to spray about her in tiny, forceful jets a clear, thin liquid, that now has covered his chest, his face, his hands, and dampened the tips of her hair.

12

If it were possible that the occupants of the house — those of the north wing as of the south, of the east as of the west — could find themselves all at the same table and, late in the evening, after a generous meal, an abundance of wine loosening their tongues, could find themselves speaking of their dreams: if this were possible, then perhaps they would discover that they held between them the substance of a story, the clue to a mystery that might help to place even if it could not complete them. But dreams, while they repair us, also fracture and divide. Dreamers know, but since what they know is locked away in dreams, and since most of their dreams are irretrievable to the waking mind, they do not know that they know.

Whether or not this is a broader phenomenon would be difficult to determine, but it is certainly a phenomenon of the house. In the west wing, at a certain level of their sleep — in a clear space where the immediate concerns of their emotions are quietened and do not cast their own confusing images — the tenants dream of texts, of labyrinths of words and pages, or else the strange, frighted figures of medieval emblem books, while those in the east find themselves trying to calm a frightened girl, a dark-haired child whose skin is the colour of almond-flesh and whose terror is never truly named, but displaced always into smaller things — a cat (that is Michael's dream), a bird (that is Mme Bloch's), a statuette (that is Axel Ségur's). But the distinctions, the particular areas of dream are not always so clear. For those in the south wing — at the moment the Pizacs and Mme Lecault, but how many have there been before them? — it is the dreams of conversations, as each translates into the terms of their own lives some dispiriting tract or another of a seemingly interminable argument in which a woman is explaining to a man who will not listen or, if the dreamer is a man, a woman will not countenance an explanation, will not forgive. But these dreams, as do the others, drift out over other parts of the house, would not be unrecognisable to those in the west or north or east; and there are yet others so ancient or so deeply connected to the place that they know no particular locality, but roam like household demons or lares and penates through the bedrooms of successive generations: the dream of the marshes, the bound woman, the swords half-buried in mud; the dream of the boat, far out on a lake, the cloaked man poling it toward the island — or is it the castle, on the far side? — and the lady shrouded, the small bundle beside her.

13

Michael tells Thérèse of the repugnance he began to feel on the day when she wet herself in the classroom. She asks him if he still feels it, and, when he says no, asks him to prove it. It is a dare, of course, and the way most of their games begin. She leads him into the bathroom and tells him to take his clothes off. She takes off her own and steps into the shower. Drawing him in, she turns on the water and they begin to play, as they have before, tickling, soaping one another, allowing wet, slippery fingers to penetrate where they might not otherwise have gone. Then Thérèse tells Michael to sit down. Straddling him, she urinates over his head and shoulders. Its taste, for he does taste it, is unexpected, not as unpleasant as he might have feared. Thin, salty, warm, a little like lemon, or the taste of his own skin.

14

Ivan Pizac has only one arm, the right, his left having been blown off to no real purpose, and his enduring bemusement, in the last weeks of the German occupation when some sticks of old and sweating gelignite thrown about in an orange-crate on the tray of a lorry, had exploded, killing the driver who only seconds before had offered him a lift. Later he was to discover that the man had been a petty collaborator, and that he had intended to use the explosives to impress the authorities by blowing-up the house of a suspected partisan. In this way, Ivan likes sometimes to think, fingers, palm, wrist, forearm, elbow, watch and a thin gold ring his father had brought with him from Ljubljana in 1913, the year before Ivan's birth, had been sacrificed for the Resistance; but the thought is never a serious one and is found, when it is found, most often in the last inch or so of a second or third bottle of wine.

It is not entirely clear, in any case, how lost the arm is. It is certainly not physically present in the sense that it could pick up a pair of pliers or hold a fork, or brace the carburettor while the air-filter is undone, but although in this way it is ten years gone its messages still continue. Still, at various intervals of the day, Ivan can feel his invisible fingers brushing the freshly polished duco of a car, or clutching an icy glass, or helping to roll a hen onto its back to stroke its breast feathers. Still, lying in his bed at night, they seem to reach out and touch Marguerite, finding her sometimes as she is now, at other times just as she was — the taut base of the belly, skin tight over the hip bones — in the years before they were blown away.

He has tried, often, to work out in what realm the lost arm exists — whether in the past, say, in which it had once felt and acted, or in some different aspect of the present — but the question seems unanswerable. Several of the things it tries to tell him could only be a part of memory, but others belong as much to the life he is now leading, the telephone he answers, the paper he shuffles in the office, now that he is no longer of much use in the garage.

There are also feelings he cannot put a name to, and these intrigue him most, shapes and surfaces he cannot identify, sensations of warmth and cold, dryness and moisture which seem to have a particular pattern to them. There are even aches, or stabs of a quite specific pain, as if just now, suddenly, he has gashed the index finger on a knifeblade, or bruised the thumb with a hammer. But how? Why? What, in its other, separate, invisible life, had he been doing? At any hour of the day or night he is likely in this way to find himself in two places at once, a place that is very much here and now, and another place, utterly unknown to him, in which he is blind, in which he has no sense but touch, but which, could he find the concentration or the secret, he could move through, discover, like another life he might be leading, something else that he might be being, other than what he is.

And what about Auguste, who has only one eye? Does he have ghost visions? Is he able to close his lost eye when he sleeps? Or does it add another dimension to his dreams? Are his visions, if he has them, whole scenes, or only partial things, colours, lines? Are they from the present or the past? Ivan tried at one point to ask, but at the slightest mention of his lost eye the gardener had grown angry and stormed off, and has scarcely spoken to him since.

Marguerite, too, has lost a part of herself, or had it taken, but to speak of this in any but the most roundabout way seems beyond them both. It is at this point that Ivan's speculations usually come to an end. Who but the woman herself can know what feeling a lost womb, lost ovaries, how many lost children might convey?

15

It is the middle of Autumn. There is still warmth in the sun, but when the sun departs there is a new chill in the air that leads to the first lighting of hearth fires, the first thoughts of winter casseroles and stews, the airing of additional blankets for the beds. The Professor has quit his desk and come downstairs for the evening. Quickly, almost automatically, as if he has done it a hundred times, he has prepared a dark sauce of Kalamata olives, anchovies, garlic, black pepper, tomatoes, and left it to simmer on the stove. Now, at the window, the first strains of Barber's adagio stirring silently in his consciousness, a prelude to the actual music, he is watching the early brewings of a storm high over the southern wing, thinking of the arrangements there of light and cloud, the last spars of sun and the welling bruise, the soon-to-be-thunder. A shipwreck, he thinks, or a projection, a dream of one — that, or sorcery, although *sortilege* might be the better term, a mixture of hazard and the law, a recognition of the rule, the sovereignty of sky.

Thinking of the angels of Rilke, and of Stéphane Mallarmé, but also of something else, something that he can't quite remember, he turns to the pan — it has been only a matter of minutes — and, resisting the temptation of the one dried chili, adds a sprinkling of capers, then places over a higher flame a pot of water for the spaghetti, adding a drop of oil, a small pinch of salt. *Puttanesca* this, a matter of whores, but also of small boys, apprentices, Piero della Francesca . . .

Cheese. That's what it was. Parmesan. Marble-textured where the knife had cut. Hard as a rock. *Finely grated, Miss Rilke, a small mountain! Where amongst the angelic hierarchies was that?*

Tell *that* to Madame Klossowska!

16

There must be a story to the plank, but if there is then no one seems to know it. It turns up in the courtyard one morning — at least that is when Mme Ségur first notices it, leaning against the wall beside her door. Although M. Ségur has his head in the clouds (as they say) and doesn't appear to notice, Hélène is curious. She goes to see whether Mme Lecault knows where it might have come from, and the concierge returns with her. About two metres long — just over the height of an ordinary man — it is a fairly new, fairly ordinary plank, slightly scuffed and dusty, but in such a way as might have occurred in any carpenter's or plasterer's storeroom. Very likely a workman has left it, but there is no work being or to be done, at least for the moment. Certainly Mme Lecault has not arranged for any. The Christophes' stairwell has been mended, as have the step in the Professor's and the attic in the Blochs', each now several weeks ago. It may have been left behind, of course, but if so neither M. Bloch nor the Professor knows anything about it. Eventually there is nothing else to do but to ask Auguste to take it to the shed, but he — it is the second day now — is busy with something in the garden and can not or will not come until evening.

By the time he arrives for it the plank is gone. He goes to Mme Lecault, whom he suspects has become impatient and arranged something else, but this time it is she who knows nothing. A mystery. Although perhaps not to everyone, or not entirely. Miklus, should anyone think to ask him (and nobody does), would at least be able to say that as he returned to his apartment at about four he had seen, while fumbling at his front door for his keys, a man leaving the courtyard with just such a board on his shoulder. He could not see the face; the board had obscured it; but there had been something familiar about him none the less, though whether it was the arm, the hand, the white pants, the shoes — whether, indeed, it was something from this reality at all, and not merely a figure from a painting he had seen (a Crucifixion by Piero? by Pantaleone?) — he couldn't, for the life of him, say.

17

One night Tad has a vision of the impossible. That is, he calls it a vision, to himself, because there is no other way of explaining it. But he is certainly not sleeping; he has not even gone to bed. It is a candle, moving from one end of the east wing to the other, its light now seen passing slowly across one window, then as slowly across the next — and then, perhaps afraid that a watcher might still be doubting it, moving slowly back in the opposite direction. If he didn't know just how impossible it was he'd say that a person was trapped there or looking for something they had lost, moving effortlessly through the walls that separate the apartments as if not only they but their occupants, their furniture — the wardrobes, the double beds, the tables and chairs and bookcases — were not there at all. Watching it return toward the room from which it had started, he finds himself counting off the windows of the various apartments: two for the Countess, two for the Professor, two for the Barbers. But something is wrong. After the sixth window the candle passes across a seventh, where surely no other window is.

It is a dark night. The moon, if there was one, has already set. As if passing now into a room for which there is no window, the candle vanishes and does not reappear. There is nothing Tad can do. Next morning, oversleeping and having to dress while still only half awake, he has already sat down to his breakfast before he remembers. His mother looks at him askance and says nothing. His sister laughs and tells him he is going mad. His father smiles and passes off the vision as a dream. Finishing his coffee, he leads Tad into the living room and, using his stump as if it were an entire arm, holding back the curtain with his other, counts out the windows on the wing in question. There are, of course, only six. One, two, three, four, five, six.

18

There is a tension, an agony, that no one is admitting, though it seems impossible that they can not feel it. A supreme agony, a joke, of universal, unbelievable proportions. Looking out his window late one afternoon Lucien Christophe sees his daughter sitting on the steps he has come to regard as hers. She is wearing a new dress that her grandmother — Madelaine's mother — has just sent her. Thérèse pretends that these things do not matter, that she does not care for them, but it's clear that she is waiting to be seen. Perhaps by Michael, or by Catherine, or by the Professor or Madame Lecault. With dismay he sees her adjusting the folds of the skirt, ensuring that, although she might be admired, she will not also be exposed. He tries to think when this began, how it might have been prevented, but in every direction that he casts he finds only paradox, fear and oppression that can not be relieved, guilt that can not allow itself to be forgiven.

Madelaine once told him that the eyes of men are like hooks, that everywhere she went she could feel them, in her arms, her back, her thighs. She sometimes wondered whether the constant presence of the eyes of men had determined the way she thought, the way her mind worked, knowing always that the body within which she lived, within which she walked, would be watched, would always have to be defended. Whatever else there was in her head, she said, there was always also this. And yet how could she escape it, what else could she do? The only alternatives were to hide, to deprive herself, or to draw even greater attention by becoming consciously different, by not wearing the clothes that a woman wears, by deliberately making herself ugly. She had said this many times, in many different ways, and always there had been a kind of hopeless accusation, as if she knew that he was trapped also, and that there was nothing adequate he could say.

Her dying, leaving him alone to tell or not to tell Stéphane, to tell or not to tell Thérèse, had only made things worse. This morning, buying a lettuce in the greengrocer's, he had looked up to see a woman his age on the other side of the stand. Her dress, beneath her coat, had a plunging neckline, and in the brief moment that his eyes had been drawn to the deep cleft between her breasts she had looked up and seen him looking, and had cast an angry glance as she turned away. It was then that he had remembered the fishhooks, but with an anger that was no less at her than at himself, at what it was that had made her wear such a dress and yet resent the attention it drew. It was as if he was perpetually divided, the mind pulling one way, the body another, insisting that he continue to do what he felt he should not, what all he knew said that he should not. Before the mind could arrest them, his eyes would seek out, pry, intrude, wounding at the very moment they seemed to answer or caress, as if merely in living he wounded, or the laws which created the conscience, the guilt, were not the laws of the body.

Sometimes, at the worst times, he *sees* that he is evil, but he does not know where the evil has come from, why it should have settled upon him. He resents this, deeply, but there seems no way out. Even in loving his own children as he does there is this dividedness, this fear.

19

It is not Hell but the Garden itself that Michael shows to Thérèse — that, and the Earthly Paradise. They wonder at the huge fruits the people eat, at the great berries that so many carry about on their heads, at the magical towers that surround the lake, and guess at the strange creatures — griffons, perhaps, or manticores — that the men are riding and the balancing games they are playing in the tight circular formations. But there is something missing; the picture is not as exciting as when Michael first looked at it. Even some of the naked people themselves seem to be standing around awkwardly now, as if they are not quite sure why they are there, or are puzzled by what others are doing. And there are other questions, other things that they leave unsaid, though perhaps for each of them, Michael and Thérèse, these are different things.

20

Almost a month passes before Mme Berry appears again, although her smile and what seems a new openness put Mme Lecault's apprehensions immediately to rest. It is not that the last of the barriers has fallen — far from it! — but small details nevertheless do sometimes now slip past her guard. There is talk, for example, of a wine cellar somewhere beneath the house, and of a subterranean passage leading to it. This is news to Mme Lecault. There is indeed a cellar to the new house, her house, that is used by the tenants as a storage space, but it is only the one large room and there is nothing leading off it. And when, her curiosity aroused, she goes down to inspect the brickwork for signs of variation, of some ancient sealing-off, she finds nothing.

There is talk, too, of a room upstairs that has not been opened for years. Mme Berry had asked several times for the key, for fear of the rats that might breed there, but the General had always refused, claiming that the cats, which even then roam so freely about the place, would look after any vermin. Eventually, without ever reopening the room itself, he had bricked-up the short passage that led to it and would never hear mention of it again. From the sounds of it, Mme Lecault deduces, this mysterious room must have been on the north side of the building, at the end, but Mme Berry can not or will not help her with more. North, South, East and West, she says, have never meant anything to her, and the building has in any case changed so much. It is the General she has been trying to explain, not the house; the room itself was locked up well before she came.

It might, she speculates, have been something from the General's childhood (he had grown up in the house), although more probably it was once the bedroom of the wife who died in childbirth scarcely a year after the marriage. The woman who had been housekeeper before her had told her that the General became very strange after that, debauched, a drunkard when not on active service, and ultimately the morose recluse she now finds herself serving. A locked room, she seems to imply, is the least of her worries. It is, after all, one less place to be dusted.

Although Mme Lecault would readily press her friend for more (had Mme Berry a husband? for there have been hints enough, or rather refusals, to suggest that her distant past is not entirely unlike Mme Lecault's own, and may even have been repressed for the same reason), it is mainly this that they talk about — the dusting, the General, the details of a severe childhood and a lonely life of service on the one hand, and the tenants, the children, events of the town on the other. Mme Lecault may not learn much of the whereabouts of the rooms her friend speaks of, but she does learn eventually their furnishings, the histories of this piece or that, and for Mme Berry, as she often says, it is as if a prayer for a companion, a friend of her own age and station has been answered: her loneliness in the big house has been oppressive.

If less and less of the time is spent in talking of the old house, it is only because so much less happens there — or so is the impression Mme Berry seems concerned to convey. Certainly it is not through Mme Lecault's desire, although ironically the desire increases thereby. Slowly, as time goes on, Mme Berry displays a stronger and stronger interest in the life ahead of her time, and an extraordinary ability to comprehend and cope with it, even at times to advise upon it, if only in the abstract. Slowly too, she loses some of her physical shyness, no longer trying so nervously to avoid the accidental touch, no longer stepping away if, as increasingly she does, Mme Lecault moves, lightly, to embrace her upon greeting, secretly surprised each time, and for all the evidence to the contrary, to find actual fabric, actual flesh.

The next time, after a long yet impatient interval, that Mme

Lecault raises the question of a closer look at the rooms her companion has been speaking of, it is as if Mme Berry has been half expecting it and is somewhat better prepared. Indeed it is she herself who now speaks of how sad it is that the traffic between them has been so much in the one direction only, and that Mme Lecault cannot visit her to see some of the lonely splendour of the place before it fades any further. Much to her friend's surprise, she now acquiesces readily to the suggestion that they take each other's hand, and that she try to lead her through.

Slowly, steadily they rise, take hands, and move across the room. Slowly, steadily, as if the wall itself were a frightable animal, they approach the place where Mme Berry has always disappeared. And slowly, steadily, only Mme Berry does so, her head, her shoulder, her arm progressively vanishing as her right hand draws Mme Lecault nearer and nearer the wall, only to disappear entirely as the too-real fingers, the too-real knuckles touch the plaster.

21

9/ix/55

A young man has come to see me, as doubtless you have intended. Is this a test, a punishment? He tells me that you gave him my name and address, that you told him much about me. It is clear that you have stopped short at many places, but it is also clear that there have been hints, ambiguous signs enough to make him wonder. Ostensibly he wishes to talk about music, but it is always you he returns to. He tells me that you walk together often around the city at night, long walks between the bridges and around the university, and that you talk endlessly. He tells me — *searching my face for a reaction* — *that you will kiss no one on the lips*, mentions it so often that it is clear that he burns to do so, and that he has at least once been rejected. He speaks especially of one night when you walked almost to Beliéres, but although he has begun upon this more than once he backs away from it, as if there were something he wishes to confess, or know, but cannot bring himself to mention.

Ironically we have done much the same, he and I, walking along the chilly boulevards and around the empty squares for four nights now, since I cannot seem to get rid of him and Denise, who says she has had enough of my students (and it was as a student that he first introduced himself), will not have him in the apartment. I believe I encourage him in order to hear of you, although it is never I who mentions your name, and although I say nothing of what I know — although, often enough, you well to my lips and I have literally to bite you down.

Last evening we went to a café where there is often a singer. It was late. There was no one at the piano and there were few customers — the season for such places is long over. It seemed that the café would close once we left, although the waiter did not hurry us, contenting himself with polishing the glasses and entering the receipts. Your friend sat down and played a piece I did not recognise, haunting and full of desire. A short piece, which he then played again, almost as if to ensure that it worked its full effect on me or that I committed it to memory. Clearly it was his own composition, and as full of you as any of his conversation. This morning, thinking about it, I have begun to write something of my own.

You have sent him to me, but what am I to do? Again I find myself confronting the long, appalling chain of desire, each of us turning away from the other, passing on our own suffering to the one who looks toward us; none of us able to do anything about it. There must be a place where *it stops, but that is almost as frightening to contemplate. There must be peace. I have always thought it would somehow settle upon me within the next few years, the next decade of my life, but years and decades have already come and gone, and while there are sometimes long stretches of contentment there is also still the brooding, the storm always threatening to break.*

22

It is 11 a.m., but at this time of year it takes the sun that long to penetrate the ground floor kitchens and bathrooms on the east side of the building. Marguerite Pizac likes to bathe once or twice a week at just this time, and this morning in particular has been impatient for the moment to arrive, so as to retire into the brief peace of water and the light that, weak as it is, shines off the clean white tiles, the scrubbed porcelain, the white paint about the window and door and mirror cabinet — so clean, so white this morning, and the day so unseasonally bright, that she opens the window, as she has not done since summer, to let the warmer air circulate.

She has been angry from the moment she woke, a foul, spitting mood, and has known it, snapping at Ivan for no reason, impatient with the children, rough and noisy with the things in the kitchen, brusque with Mara to a point where she actually cried. Now, lying in the tepid water, scooping it over her neck and face, she tries to locate the cause and thinks eventually of the dream that she woke from, an old dream of betrayal and humiliation that goes back as far as she can remember. It has never occurred to her before that there might be a connection between dreams and the actual mood you carry into the day, but perhaps that is it — an upsetting thought, if you consider that you don't often remember your dreams, so that over and over again you might have moods you cannot remember the cause of.

And where, anyway, did that dream come from in the first place? It could be as far away as childhood, but she can think of nothing bad enough to have caused it. Could her anger be so old that it is reaching up from something twenty or thirty years ago, something that can never now be known? Or even that it is something she has inherited, something even older than she is? And her fear, then — this persistent, unshakeable conviction that something is wrong, that still nothing can explain — can that be the same? By now she is prepared to think almost anything.

After the feeling itself, that is almost the worst part about it, the thinking, the way she can not get it out of her mind. The way she has been catching herself, over and over in the weeks since it began, sitting in the semi-darkness of the living room, with her tea gone cold, and realising that she has been like that for an hour or more, neglecting her work, getting almost nothing done before Ivan comes home. But she has tried everything she can and has still come up with nothing. Or, if you look at it another way, with so many things, but not one of them adequate, not one of them right. She has even written letters. She has even read the newspaper. But the people she has written to have already answered cheerily, with delight and surprise and puzzlement at having heard from her. And the papers, although as full as ever of shocking things, have offered nothing that has not already happened so many times that it could not be the answer at all. She suspects, anyway, that whatever it is that is wrong is not the sort of thing that one finds in newspapers, that it is more like one of those things the doctors don't or won't know, outside any such system of description or measurement. As if everything has a double meaning, but nothing can help you understand what the second one is.

Stepping out of the bath, beginning to towel herself dry, she catches sight of her body in the mirror, something that normally she tries not to do. As a rule, in any case, the steam mists the glass, making reflection impossible. Today, however, with the window open, it has remained clear, and she can see in appalling detail the ugly, battered nakedness she usually so carefully avoids, the scar where she had that operation as a girl when her appendix burst; the scar where they took out Tad; the larger scar where they took out Mara and so much else, without asking or even saying; the scar where they operated again to try to fix what they had caused — pale, tough patches of skin that have not stretched like the rest, and so have caused deep ravines in her belly and abdomen, beneath the breasts that have sagged, the chin that has doubled, the upper lip upon which there is a more and more noticeable moustache, the eyes in their deepening rings of tiredness. This horrid thing, this revolting thing she is now forced to live in.

She had said something to Tad. He came into the bedroom one time when she was dressing — just as she had taken off her nightgown — and pointed, and asked. 'You did that to me', she said, unable to control herself, even taking a sort of pleasure in his bewilderment. But it has nothing to do with him. She felt bad about it even as she was saying it, but was unable to stop herself, could not take it back. Sometimes these things come up out of you, boil up out of nowhere. It was the doctors, not Tad. It was not even Ivan, with his fat, stubby, relentless hammer of a thing.

The way he would bruise her, no matter how gentle he tried to be. It is the doctors, but then also it isn't them either. And yet of course it is. In some way they are all involved.

23

Michael has a dream that makes him afraid. He and Thérèse are together, and they begin their game in the usual way, although this time there is a special excitement, a greater urgency, and they soon go further than they have ever gone before. There are hard, cold edges, hot blind places, pleasures that are so great that they become real pain. It is not dark, but they are so close together, so lost in skin and taste and perspiration that it is difficult to know what they have done or might be doing. They were naked and then the flesh somehow engulfed or entangled them. It was hard to tell which part of them was him, or which part was her. Then, suddenly, there is a warm, red, shining liquid all over and between them. And a sudden terror, an urge to scream that cannot become sound, a suffocating thrashing that turns just as abruptly into the cool room, the darkness, the bedsheets twisted and his heart racing and the night breeze gently lifting and dropping the curtain over the open window.

It is after this he gives Thérèse the mirror. It's not that there is a special connection in his mind, nor even that there is any particular memory of the magic he once thought it possessed. Rather, it is out of fear that unless he gives her some such solid thing she might drift away, or that they might both lose reference, fall, float too far free from anything they might yet come back to. Although when he comes to see her again and finds her lying dreamily on the couch, her skirt raised and her legs stretched out, staring at her own face in the mirror, failing completely to notice or acknowledge him, he begins to think that it is too late.

Perhaps he would think this all the more if he could see her afterwards, with her paint set, sitting cross-legged with her underpants off and the mirror propped in front of her, painting what she sees there: a vast winter landscape, an avenue of tall trees, thick with branches, every twig distinct, stark against the pearled, pale orange of the sky. The deep, rutted road.

This is not the end, not truly, although it is not clear to Michael what is or what could be. The summer holidays are long over and the renewed contact with her other friends seems to have drawn her away from him. Several times, when he goes to see her, he finds her with Katia or Louise Bouvier and feels quite deliberately excluded. At other times — especially, it seems, when a sort of urgent need has arisen in him to see her and to play one of their games — Thérèse is simply not at home, as if the force of his need itself has somehow determined her absence. After almost a month has gone by and he has not been able to see her alone there seems nothing else to conclude but that she has grown tired of him and does not want to see him. Feeling embarrassed and somehow betrayed he decides that he will not try again.

What, then, should he make of her coming to the open window while he is reading a comic in the courtyard, and staring at him so strangely that it does not seem possible to answer, continuing to stand there even when the Professor, not noticing her, stops to talk to him and he has to struggle to focus his attention, wondering for days afterward what it was that she had wanted or reminded him of — an owl, perhaps, or falcon; a creature with wings and claws and sharp, impassive eyes — and whether it was him she had been staring at at all.

24

Lucien Christophe returns to find himself squatting in the corner of the bathroom, his toes and his fingers bleeding. Cleaning the torn places, rubbing ointment into the cuts around his ankles and wrists, the two long scratches on his cheek, he puts his nightclothes on him and puts him to bed, cradling him in his arms until he sleeps. He is completely unable to determine what is the matter.

This is not the first time. There have been others when his gums, his lips have split and bled, when his fingers have told him that his ears or his navel were doing likewise. It is not intentional, not a wilful self-mutilation or devouring, at least not yet. But what other explanation could there be? There it is, the blood, on his hands, his fingers. A reminder of something he can not remember, do what he can to prevent it.

Possession revisits the possessor. Undeniably, unavoidably he becomes the possessed. There is a common theory that explains ghosts or spirits as the residue of intense emotion captured in the walls or floors or ceilings of the rooms that once witnessed it. There is another theory that such passionate excess does not return in some separate or disembodied form, but, at some unpredictable time or times later, although often in very nearly the same place, as an eruption, a surplus, in one who might never otherwise have felt it.

25

The Professor sits many hours at a time, throughout a grey morning or long grey afternoon, listening to string concerti, at first clear-headed and attentive but at some point or another resigning, becoming increasingly lost in the throbbing of the bass, the wandering of cellos, stumbling now and again into the thin clear peace of the unaccompanied harp or lute, aware that somewhere deep within this, in a place he has not yet found, a great bird is floundering in a thicket of its own past flight, thrashing, pausing sometimes in exhaustion or as if to listen to the wind in the invisible branches above it. Then emerges, the coffee long cold beside him, the tray full of butts and ashes, and, with an effort that seems almost incredible, moves. The huge, unhoused, unaccommodatably ugly body which suddenly needs to urinate, or defecate, again.

26

It was more than two years ago. He and Lisette and his sister used to play together. Lisette and Mara were best friends and for as long as Tad could remember had tried to involve him in their games, but something else had started to happen. It came to be always the same game, and always Tad would be trying to be alone with Lisette; always it would be building toward that point where he would have played it with his sister and now it would be Lisette's turn and the game couldn't finish until she had had it.

It was a wet weather game, a winter game. You could only play it in the bedroom, and only when the parents were out or too busy to want to come and see what you were doing. Sometimes they played it at Lisette's, but her mother was too friendly and was always coming to talk to them, to ask them if they wanted things. Maybe it was just that she didn't trust them. Mostly, anyway, they played it at his and Mara's.

It was called Tortures, and there were always the same rules. Sometimes he was a Gestapo man and they were partisans, and sometimes he was the partisan and they were Germans or collaborators. It didn't really matter: they would take it in turns. Sometimes the partisans would capture the Gestapo and sometimes the Gestapo would catch the partisans, but always someone was captured and had a secret and the others would be trying to get it out of them. They wouldn't give up the secret and had to be tortured. The secret was important for a while — at least, you had to pretend that it was — but the torture was always the point of it. And it never was real torture anyway.

You had to have the proper kind of secret, a complicated one with lots of parts, so that it would take several questions and admissions to get all of it out. And you had, too, to apply the right kinds of torture, so that the victim wouldn't want to give in too soon. It had to be a torture that they liked, or that they liked almost as much as they didn't. Some days Lisette and Mara would like it more than others, and some days they would like it less. That's what made it unpredictable.

It had taken them a long time to work it out properly, but it had seemed to work better and better, and to last longer and longer. It depended a lot on what mood they were in. The game could be ruined if someone gave in too soon, or didn't really want to play, or if the secret was too simple. To make it work you had to balance everything out. Often you had to make deals before you started, so that everyone got what they really wanted (though nobody ever actually said what that was). Somewhere along the line he'd got the idea of pretending not to want to do some things that he actually wanted to do, and of pretending to want to do things he didn't, so that he could get his way more easily. But then somewhere along the line, too, Mara and Lisette had seemed to get the same idea. Eventually it was all part of the game. If people didn't really like what was going on there were lots of ways of stopping it, and they were all built in, so that you didn't actually have to cry about it or go running to your mother.

Some days, since there were only three of them, Mara would be on his side, and some days it would be Lisette. Most often, since they were best friends, it would be them against him. He liked it best when Mara and he were on the same side, because then he wouldn't have to torture her. It was never so much fun to torture her as it was to torture Lisette.

It didn't start off so at first, but it got more and more so it would begin with him. He would be captured, and whoever was playing the soldier or the policeman or one of the ordinary partisans would lead him in before the one who was playing the captain or the judge or the partisan leader. He would have a fairly easy secret, so as to be sure that they would get it before too long. Sometimes they would twist his arms behind his back, or give him Chinese burns, and sometimes — he would always try to make sure that he wore a belt that was done up really tightly — they would very slowly pull his pants down. But mostly — the one he liked most, and the one they always tried when the others didn't work — they would make him lie down on the floor and they would sit on him, one of them on his hands and one just below his stomach if he was lying on his back, or on his backside if he was lying the other way. And they would bounce up and down, or they would try to grind themselves down on him until he gave up.

When it was his turn to be the torturer he would do the same things. His favourite was the sitting on them, though he did this differently. He would always make them lie over the edge of the bed, and he would sit on their backsides. If he moved himself in the right way their skirts would ride up — sometimes they would even let him make this an official part of the torture — and then he would be sitting on their underpants. Slowly, asking them the questions over and over, giving them plenty of chance to give in so they could never really say that he'd forced them, he'd ride their pants down until their backside was bare. That was usually the signal for the game to end, but sometimes they still wouldn't give in and he'd have to roll them over. Sometimes, too, before their backside was completely bare, something would happen in his own pants and the game would finish anyway, because he'd say he had to go to the toilet, and would rush out, embarrassed, hoping that they hadn't seen.

Maybe that's what had eventually ruined it. It had happened more and more often, and always when he was torturing Lisette. It got to be a way that they could win the game, and that he couldn't always stop from happening, that he didn't want, but also at some point wanted to happen. Sometimes he thought that they were trying to make it happen almost as much as he. It was a hot, tense, urgent game, and there was always the danger that someone's mother or father would come in and start screaming, and they'd never be able to do it again. They knew it was wrong, somehow, the game, but they couldn't have really said why.

In the end it wasn't anyone's mother or father after all. It was them. One day he came in and they were laughing at him. They sat in a corner as his mother spoke to him about something and they were giggling — whispering, looking at him, and giggling. It was conspiratorial, but this time he was not a part of it. He was being cut out. Since then it had never been the same. No one mentioned tortures any more. They would try sometimes to get him to play some other game with them, and to be friendly again, and sometimes he would try, but always there was what they knew and couldn't unknow. For a long time now he had avoided them as much as he could. Somehow the very sight of them made him angry — all the more so because he knew it didn't make any difference, that they didn't care. And if they didn't care he wasn't going to either.

27

So much of Bernard's life and thought is spent upon his fiction that he has come to wonder if it is not the fiction that he truly lives in, and whether the man who does the banking or the shopping, who sits with friends or corresponds with publishers, agents, other writers — the living being who eats and sleeps and washes and deals with its variety of small physical needs — is not merely a carapace, an amanuensis to the text that flows from it. It seems to him that at any one point, of all the many things he does, the fiction itself and the processes of writing it are the two he knows most about. Sometimes, indeed, he seems to be so much composed by them that he wonders whether it is he who has created the fiction or the fiction that has created him.

Increasingly, too, the writing becomes its own subject. It can hardly be otherwise. It is the writing that he exists for, that occupies the best of his time. The psychology and mysteries of the process itself intrude upon and in some way shape all that he writes about. Aware of this in his own work, constantly amazed at the ways it has infiltrated the most unwriterly of his characters and events, he begins to suspect that every other book is also in some part a book about writing. For a time, in each one he reads, he finds himself looking for the point where the fiction gives away its self-absorption, its secret, inevitable narcissism.

He sometimes thinks, astonished and confused at the extravagance of the idea, that it's as if writing were the shaping force of life. Day after day he ransacks his own past for material, finding useful now the almost-forgotten scent of a flower, now the view from a certain window in his grandfather's house, now the feel, once, of the old man's hand, fresh from digging potatoes — as if all along these things had been waiting for the new existence writing would give them, and had now found a place and meaning they had not had before. Writing has thus become a way of ordering, of determining what in his life has had importance. Only through it, it sometimes seems, can he find out why some thing, some incident had had its being.

It's not immediately clear how this should influence the conduct of life, although he is sure that in some way it must. If people and things and incidents exist in order to be named and given their place and function within a story or the wider order of names, then how should he respond? Should he focus more and more on the processes of naming and ordering, to the increasing exclusion of experience itself, or should he seek wherever possible to expand his experience, so as to have all the more to bring to the fiction? Attent on the process, he risks shutting out the world.

And yet, attent on the world, mightn't he lose sight of the process?

But the dilemma is only temporary. Bernard by nature is neither profligate nor particularly adventurous, and eventually determines that as far as possible experience must not be allowed to obscure the lineaments of process — that process, in the long run, is almost all, the most significant occurrences being as they are mental ones, or those of a less definable evanescence: a politician with white hair seen once in a limousine late at night in a deserted city centre, the crook of a woman's knuckle as she bit down into it in approaching climax, a small boy coming late to the smoke-filled study, the spittle from his father's pipe, God leaving quietly, as if by a back door, while one was sleeping . . .

28

It is almost impossible to say what it is that makes some people heir to things and others not. Mme Bloch is not particularly sympathetic. She is efficient, intelligent, attractive and independent, more so than most of those she has worked for, but these, like the past and the character which sustain them, are private matters, and she is very private. Why then does it seem to her so often as if she has some secret mark upon her cheek or chin or forehead, a sign that she can not detect but that leads others, seeing it, to reveal their secrets to her, if not so much in words then in actions, glances? She has the unsettling sense — confirmed over and again by fleeting eye contact that seems as deep and as painful as it is impossible to avoid — that she knows the Countess without ever having spoken to her. She has a sense, too, whenever she and the Professor meet, that at some point in the past, wiped from her memory, he has entrusted her with a secret that need never afterward be mentioned, but that somehow separates them from those around them. A secret that, yes, she *does* know, but can scarcely mention even to herself, since it is such a large one, since it involves almost everything.

This moment, for example, when, at seven in the morning of a day after a day full of rain, of a day that promises to be no different, looking out of her bedroom window at the sky above the west wing and casting about to the north and south for some sign of a break in the clouds, she sees Lucien Christophe at his own window, naked, staring straight ahead, and can not move her eyes away from the grey-silver light that bathes the unexpected strength of the shoulders or washes the tautness of the belly she would have thought so much softer, or probes toward the glimmer of the penis in its small nest of hair. And then looking up at his face again, to find it turned to her, and an expression that, innocent and unabashed, is at once a pleading and a complicity, a recognition.

This sense that she has that they will pretend, and go on pretending, that they will know and yet act as if they don't, for the sake of all of those about them who need to think that things are different, that things are far more solid than they are.

29

It is not the end, but as if some part of a dream, a hope, has certainly vanished. And in her disappointment, her fear that the relationship has been irreparably damaged, it may be that Mme

Lecault herself goes too far. She had resolved, very early in their strange acquaintance, to say as little as possible of the history that lay between them, the past that to Mme Berry would of necessity be future, and although it is perhaps inevitable that occasional details slip through, it has become their unspoken practice to act as if they have not been heard or, if this is not possible, that what has been said simply does not make sense. But on one night there is an accident, a wrong turning, and as if despite herself, unable to turn back, Mme Lecault finds herself uttering things, raking her mind for details, making connections she had intended never to reveal, some of them even to herself.

There has been a question, the very simplest of questions, but the answer requires explanation, and that explanation another. Before she knows it Mme Lecault finds herself in a labyrinth, or rather the long, winding path that she knows — she has now, having trapped herself, to show — *does* have light, *does* have peace at the end, but that also trips one, that is fraught with forgotten explosions. The Revolution leads her inexorably to the Storming, the Storming to the execution of the King, the execution of the King to the guillotine, the Terror, the rivers of blood, and then, as if to reward, to calm, to restore vanishing hope — whether it is Mme Berry's or her own now she can no longer tell — to the Emperor and the glorious wars, but somehow these too turn to devastation and she has to struggle on further, picking her words as carefully as if they were steps over a field of corpses, watching them for the least bloody but going on and having to use some anyway, sticky, slippery with newly-spilt blood, as if each were a forearm or a just-severed foot. Napoleon leads to the Second Republic, one Empire to another. She tries to lighten the onslaught with stories of Marie Antoinette, of Napoleon and

Josephine, of Louis Napoleon and the plank he is supposed to have carried to hide his face as he escaped from the Fortress of Ham, but the blood and the horror continue unabated, nothing she knows of can stop them. Even their own quarter, their own building not escaping, Foch nailing his own hand to the cross in Notre Dame des Ifs, his night-trail of horror, the young man dead on the pavement outside, the missing girl. After the Second Empire there is Sedan and the Prussian War, and after Sedan even more: Flanders, Passchendaele, the gas and the trenches — fighting back something of her own here — the Terror not ending, the horror only darker, more wearying, and ahead, over twenty, over thirty years, only a greater horror still which she can not, she dare not name, which something will have to prevent her from naming. For she *can* not herself. Something has happened and she can not herself. She had not known this anger, this horror was in her, and now that it has begun to erupt it seems nothing can stop her.

She has not looked at Mme Berry for some time. Now, conscious that there is no light, no hope she can offer except somehow, desperately, *herself*, this, the *feel* of things, *this*, and radishes and children and the sky, lemons, *this*, she turns her red eyes toward her companion, and sees herself seen as she could only and yet could never have expected, not as one who has uttered lies, not as one who has just spewed vomit, or spoken incredible prophecy, nor even as a stranger from the future, but as a phantasm, something from nightmare, a figment of the mind — a poet's, a macabre artist's dream.

Both women sit long into the darkness. Nothing further is said. Hours later, it might be, Mme Lecault wakes stiff in her chair to find herself alone in the cold dawn. Somewhere in that other house, that other century, it is probably the same for Mme Berry.

30

In late September a letter arrives from Rio, a special event for most people perhaps, but especially for Mme Lecault, who, although by now used to those from Australia, Portugal, Belgium, Italy or Turkey, has never seen one from South America before. It is not addressed to her, of course — the inscription is to Fr. Professor Giovanni di Giovanni — but this does not lessen the pleasure of its thin, crackling, eggshell-blue envelope, its four brightly coloured stamps, or the faint but distinct scent of jungles and oceans and carnival, piranhas and peppers and flat earthen breads that she breathes deeply in as she holds it to her cheek.

Mme Lecault rarely keeps mail for more than a day. She is very scrupulous about this. But it is almost two before, reluctantly, she places this one in the appropriate pigeonhole. Even then, propped against the vinegar flask on her kitchen counter so that she could glance at it as she worked or ate, it barely escaped a soaking by spilt coffee on the second morning, and has come to bear, on its top left-hand corner, the trace of a buttery thumb. Perhaps it is only these that make her let go of it so soon, vaguely hoping as she has been that she might show it to Mme Berry, who takes delight in such small, containable windows on a later century.

The Professor receives the letter with evident pleasure, and tells her — since he sees her glance in his direction through her open door — that it is from one of his oldest friends, a monk he'd once taught with in Saint Girond, but who'd been sent first to teach at a boys' school in New South Wales and then, after the war, to South America. They'd quite lost touch, he said, until he had an idea that had led him to make enquiries. He'd written to him just after Easter, with a special request (at this point he pauses briefly but dramatically), and here, when he'd almost given up hope, had come the reply.

When he passes Mme Lecault again on his way to the markets later in the day — the Professor always goes to the markets on Friday afternoons, when the fish stalls are at their best and the vegetables freshest — she asks him whether the letter had contained all he'd wanted, hoping in her turn that the enquiry will elicit some explanation of the mysterious request. 'Yes', he says, in a tone that betokens a deep satisfaction, and leaves her, with a polite nod, no wiser than before.

31

Mme Barber is hearing things. That is, she hopes that she is, and yet hopes also that she is not. Either possibility disturbs her.

It began on a night in late summer. She awoke slowly from a dream of her husband, a dream of great loneliness in which she found herself so lost and so despairing that she had almost consciously struggled to awaken. And in the long moments in which she had done so, the long moments in which she had lain suspended, neither fully sleeping nor fully awake, she had found another loneliness, or something like it, faintly, distantly, rhythmically filling the night — a sobbing, perhaps, or it may have been no more than a throbbing of air. She had thought immediately of Catherine and, wrenching herself into a fuller consciousness, left quietly if groggily her own room to feel her way down the corridor. But it was not her daughter. Of course it wasn't. As she stood there, her ear against the bedroom door, she found the sound coming instead from somewhere above, and so began to feel her way nervously upstairs. But the third bedroom — the guestroom, as she had come to think of it, although there had never as yet been a guest — was empty. She stood in the dark and listened further. The sound was coming from behind the wall: impossibly, since on that side was only the Professor; but then the possible, the plausible, seemed to have little to do with it. A crying, an infant's crying (and yet surely it had not been an infant before?), rhythmical, insistent, inexplicable, hollow, as if there were no one there to comfort it, as if nobody ever would. And yet there was — there is — no infant in the house. Children, yes, but none so young as this. And the cry is not even like Catherine's as she remembers it.

When asked tentatively the next morning, Catherine herself said that she had heard nothing, and her mother did not pursue it. But the sound has not gone away. Although for weeks at a time, often for a month or more, she does not hear it, it seems to wait for her, as if sometimes in a dream or as she drifts off to sleep a door in her mind has been left ajar, or a window open, or the flue of a fireplace, so that the sound can travel up the chimney, through a wall-space, across the courtyard of a house as much real as it is unreal, unreal as it is real. Several times, unable to turn back into sleep, drawn on the leash of sound, she rises and climbs the stairs and sits in the dark or into the blue, grainy light of dawn, at first torn, wrenched from herself, longing to comfort, and perhaps *for* it, and then calm, almost mesmerised, as if, summoned, ancient things have arisen within her before which she sits helpless: awe-struck and utterly helpless.

32

Thérèse is sitting in her accustomed place on the courtyard steps, watching a pigeon that is itself watching a beetle that is itself, perhaps, watching a mite as it watches something even smaller. A thought strikes her. Several. She turns and looks carefully about her, trying hard to see behind the patches of sky or lemon tree or tiny Thérèse-face reflected in the panes. No one is watching. At least, not as far as she can tell.

The thoughts are these: that a pigeon can go where she herself can not. That, especially, it can take things, if they are small enough, up into the sky. That it could lift the beetle, say, over the roofs, and that things must look very different from up there, very small and strange and insignificant. And that perhaps, if she could load all the people from the house onto a pigeon's back, or make them for a moment into birds, they could all see the house differently, although not of course themselves.

If she could get some birdseed, and find a spell, and whisper into it all the things to be taken away — her father's worry, the Professor's sorrow, whatever it is that makes Mme Ségur stand looking so blankly out the window, or Michael so urgent, so sensitive — and sprinkle it out on the paving stones, and watch as the pigeons ate it, and then frighten them so that they rose up and flew into the sky . . .

33

They are in a large central hall of an institution. Huge, like an empty warehouse or the great waiting room of an abandoned railway station, it could be a prison, or hospital; it could be an asylum. Light floods in where the heavy drapes have been drawn from the large, arched windows at the farther side, but much of the rest is dim, almost musty. Everyone is dressed in drab clothing, browns and greys, and groups and individuals are moving about listlessly. Several are sitting on plain institutional chairs, not talking, staring into middle distances, their minds apparently blank or preoccupied with their own inner worlds. They — he and the woman — are sitting on a bench against the wall, beside an old man who is sleeping and who smells strongly of stale urine. The woman is sitting on his lap, or straddling it, her back to him. Her dress is rucked up, and he is inside her. She is rocking very slowly back and forth, her back slightly arched, now grinding her sex and her buttocks downward with a slow and fierce deliberation, now softening, releasing, rising slightly, or sitting tensely still as if to feel the blood's pulse in his penis deep within her as it builds to near climax and then — so deeply do they seem to be attuned — recedes, is quietened, only to build again. They are watching the sad parade, lost at once in it and in their own bodies, the warm, numbing ecstasy of the fluid between them. No one seems to have noticed them or what they are doing. Or perhaps it is only that this is not particularly unusual, or that no one cares.

Later — in the same dream, perhaps, or in another — they are in the same room, but the bench has become a stage. There is still some listless movement about the hall, though most of the people are seated. Now they are lying down, he and the woman, and people are watching. There is no noise, no evident interest, though as he approaches climax, as he senses it building in her, he senses it also in the hall at large, a leaning, an almost imperceptible tensing like a surreptitious tide within the passive bodies about them. Worlds merge. Or rather the skin between them, drawn so tight, ruptures; night and the body, the sudden, real darkness and the dream collide. Wrenching himself, with a familiar urgency, from the room and the stares, trying desperately to hold on to the image and the feel of her, Lucien rolls onto his back and throws the bedclothes aside, struggling to open his eyes to the grey winter light.

Waking properly, rinsing himself with tepid water in the icy bathroom, he finds with a kind of shamed frustration that he can not remember who she was. Her face had been so intimate, so familiar, as of his wife or a dear friend, but she was neither of these, and now it is gone.

Later, fastening his collar at the courtyard window, he looks down to see the Countess leaving her apartment, the long black skirt, the distinctive red cross on the crown of her hat, the slender, elegant fingers. It is her.

The Orangery

1

A sudden shriek and scuttering of cats. Some tom caught in coitu. Night bristling with their heat. At first Axel lies there, hoping to drift back to sleep, but unable to do this he rises and goes for a glass of water, not turning on lights lest they disturb Hélène, who has somehow slept through, or awaken him irreversibly from the dream he hopes to return to.

Slowly, as stands there sipping, staring drowsily into nothingness, thinking only of the cold, delicious liquid and the freeing of his dry, sleep-hardened mouth, his eyes become accustomed to the dark and he finds himself conscious of a lighter place, or rather that it is such a place that he has been staring at, a paleness coming from the foot of the attic stairs. Carefully he feels his way to them and begins to ascend, the lightness increasing perceptibly as he does so.

From the half-open door of the upstairs room — the room they have long since ceased to call the Nursery — a cool but intense blue is emanating. He approaches and, pushing the door more fully open, steps inside. The entire room is suffused by the same blue light, deepest and brightest at the edges of the motionless angels. It does not, however, seem to come from them. Rather, it clings to their surfaces as iron filings cling to a magnet. Motionless, utterly silent, he stands there watching, perhaps for an hour or more, until — or, rather, 'and then' — he again awakens, in his own bed, beside Hélène, with the ringing of the seven o'clock alarm, convinced — aware — that he has been, is being, will continue to be visited, and faintly afraid of what it is that such a thing might mean.

2

Michael has decided to return the postcard and the prints in person. Some of the reasons he would find hard to explain, though clearly one is a wish to see again the large print of the Garden on the Professor's study wall, and another the desire to ask, if the opportunity arises, some one or another of the questions that the triptych has repeatedly called up in him: why is there such darkness and violence in Paradise? why do people look so bored in the Garden of Worldly Delights? how can people be taking such pleasure in Hell?

The Professor greets him warmly and invites him in. He fusses for a moment over what he might offer him — there is no cake, but there may be some cheese or an apple; there is only a little milk, but perhaps he would like tea, or some bottled water — and is visibly grateful when Michael says that he is not hungry or thirsty, but would like instead to see the picture. The light in the stairwell works now and as they climb the narrow flight, the Professor motioning him to go first and then labouring up heavily behind him, Michael can see the etchings more clearly. Something about the middle one seems different, and he would pause at it were it not for the old man's evident discomfort as he follows. The study door is closed. As he steps back to allow the Professor to open it — feeling that it would be somehow impertinent to do so himself — he finds himself leaning on a narrow, third door that he does not remember noticing before. He has barely time to register this, however, before the Professor motions him in. For some minutes they stand in silence before the print, each of them seeming to take as much pleasure from it as the other. The colours of this garden are far more intense than those in the postcards. In this, as in almost all other respects, the print is much as Michael remembers it. But for the eyes. It might be nothing more than the effect of the light — coming now, as it is, from a different source and angle (it is already almost dark outside, and the Professor has turned on the reading lamp) — but he cannot remember having seen before so many eyes turned toward him; blank or startled, without recognition, but none the less as if it were on him and him alone that they focused.

Perhaps it is this that unsettles him enough to pause, as they descend, by the second of the etchings in the stairway. And to realise. The old man who had been standing on the steps of the temple is gone, and the temple doors are closed. Clearly it is not the same picture as was there before, but a companion piece. Has the Professor exchanged them? When they reach the ground floor he asks, and receives a look of such puzzlement that he feels he should repeat the question. 'No', the Professor says, almost impatiently, 'I have changed nothing. There have always been only the three of them. There was never a man there. It must have been your imagination, or the poor light before Auguste changed the bulb. What a strange thing! There was never a man there.'

Michael is hurt by the Professor's tone. It is as if the old man has been suddenly reminded that he is talking to a child and is embarrassed that he had ever thought otherwise. It is only a moment, and the Professor is kind enough as he shows Michael out. But the door does close, this door too, and Michael is left not only with the disappointed realisation that he has not asked the questions he came with, but feeling also the victim of a kind of injustice. The man *was* there, the door *had* been open, whatever the Professor had chosen to say, and the Professor must have known it. Later, as Michael lies in bed, thinking over what has happened, the unanswered questions multiply. If the man had been there, and was not any longer, where is he, which way did he go?

3

All dreams are peculiar, it may be, although it may be also that the dreams of the chronic insomniac are of a particular kind. Certainly, for Mme Lecault, those that come on the crest of long wakefulness — in the delicious, dawn-straddling hours when sleep finally arrives — have an intensity unmatched in the dreams of any other time. An intensity, although it may also be a kind of beatitude. Now and again, in any case, Mme Lecault has found, at the far end of an episode of her exhausted and exhausting sleeplessness, a place, rather than a person, though whether it is a dream or a crossing — so thin, by then, are the borders — she could not say.

This, for example, in which she finds herself — for all dreams, subject as they are to recurrence, occupy a kind of perpetual presence — sitting by a window in the corner of a large room (a sixth sense tells her that it should be a kitchen, though there is little evidence of this) not unlike the room in which she has just drifted off, waiting for someone to open the great wooden door. As if she were a child — she is a child — and the person for whom she waited were a mother, an aunt. She is there for a long time. Sometimes she thinks she dozes, her head on the sill. Birds cross the open window. She watches them dart and swirl, two of them, against a blue rectangle of sky. Although the room itself with its stone walls and its dark stone floor is cool, a warm breeze drifts over her, stirring the heads of the pinks, the cornflowers, the tiny carnations that in a vase on the little wicker table beside her smoulder in the half-light.

She is becoming restless. What does it mean, when you dream that you are naked? She has been told that she must not move. She knows that the door is not locked, however, and that were she to go to it and to pull it open she could see outside. Eventually this is exactly what she does. The light — she has dragged it open, the door heavier, stiffer than she thought — pours in upon her like a palpable force, a strong wind or a large burning hand placed on her child's forehead, pushing her back, temporarily blinding her to anything but white.

Trees and grass appear, and then an old cart, then slowly, beyond them, a wide archway in an ancient stone wall, a path, open fields, a distant steeple. And on the path, coming just now into view, a woman — is it Mme Berry? — holding the hand of a child, a girl with long, dark hair like her own. A kind of heat haze still separates them. Try as she might she can not force her eyes to gather the child's features. Only the grasses, the blare of light, the opening, the whelming of an immense sorrow that she had not known was there.

4

17/xi/55

No. You ask why I have done this to you, but don't you know that we also do these things to ourselves? Neither of us has options, and what I so often to my shame have to admit I must have somehow done to you, though also been unable to help, another voice within me protests has also been allowed, invited, as if there were some part of you that accepted its likelihood, with open eyes. If neither of us can leave (even if it is only this strange room in our minds), it seems foolish to blame one another. You can, and do, take your pleasure elsewhere. And I do also. And for all its blackness and pain I think we somehow 'take our pleasure' in this too.

Would it have gone on so long if we were together, in the one country, the one city, the one house? I doubt it. One can only stand so much intensity, and I think we must have destroyed it, or ourselves, sooner, not later. So why is it that neither of us has taken advantage of distance to end it? It is almost as if we have chosen to love, objectless (if love is what it is!). We write now to the ideas of each other. I wonder, sometimes, if the intensity of my desire to see you, to touch you, to smell you again, to enter you, to be entered by you, is not merely a desire to verify that you are there, that you are not greatly different from the you to whom I write, of whom I think, for whom I compose, for I don't see how you can be. And sometimes, reading your letters to me, I think that in the person you blame, as in the person you reject — the person who clutters the letters you receive with things that are 'not written to you' — I can see an idea of me that I at once struggle to be and yet know also I am not, and can not be.

Maybe that is it; maybe we are each trying to reach something beyond ourselves. As if this flesh were a dream through which, if pressed, if taken to extremes, we can sometimes detect the lineaments of something else, more durable, larger. As if the lover — the actual lover — blocks our vision, obscures the horizon. Without each other to crash, to exhaust ourselves upon, mightn't it be that the waves of our desire continue, go on and on, and we can learn something about them that we could never learn otherwise?

5

At last the door is unlocked and he is able to pass through into a huge, dark room crammed with books from floor to ceiling on all sides, illuminated only dimly by what light filters down from four tiny, high windows that are themselves almost entirely obscured by volumes on their sills. It is not in this house, his own house — how could it be? — yet in the dream there is no question that it is. Thick dust, when he touches the books, coats even their spines, and the atmosphere, the mustiness, is oppressive. He none the less lingers over volume after volume, amazed as much by what he recognises as what he has never seen or heard of before, finding alike answers to questions he has long puzzled over and mysteries he has, to his amazement, never yet thought to contemplate, though their significance is now so obvious and their resolution so crucial. He can scarcely believe the things he holds in his hands: priceless first editions, items centuries old, books thought to have been lost forever, ancient and beloved texts in the forms and bindings in which they first appeared. Eventually — bewildered, his mind bursting with a hundred passages, references, ideas he must somehow remember — he reaches a door at the far end and, finding it also unlocked, passes into a room identical to the anteroom from which he had at first entered: the same engraving, the same lamp, the same carpet and desk. He sits down at the huge, handwritten volume that is arranged as always as if awaiting him, and, taking up the pen, finds not only that he can now read the script that before had been indecipherable, but that, in a hand indistinguishable from the hand that had just been writing, he is able to continue the unfinished sentence with an uncanny knowledge of where it is to go. He writes as if possessed, or taking dictation from a voice that only his hand can hear, and as he writes he is pulled inward, downward, toward the things he had somehow always known would be there: the huge, dark bird with the monstrous wings, the murder of the infants, the terror on the rocky hillside, the desecration of the temple, the pestilence, the men eating excrement, the defilement of women . . .

6

At first it was the coffee, tasting of petrol, and then the sour wine. And there had also been dreams, last week of tall buildings with huge, pale, snake-like monsters waving blindly about from the tops of them, and now, last night, of Axel — at least she thought it was Axel — paying uncommon attention to her nipples, exciting her as such attention had never done before, over and again to the brink of orgasm. All day her breasts had felt uncommonly sensitive, full, as if, although she had woken, although she had risen and showered and dressed, the dream had continued within her.

It has become increasingly evident to Hélène Ségur that she is pregnant. Just as she had begun to think that she was beyond such a possibility. Just as she might have presumed that the absence of a period meant something else. And long — cruelly long — after they had given up hope. Far from the joy she might once have expected there is now only a dull sense of irony. That, and something occasionally very close to panic.

She does not tell Axel. At least not yet. There are several reasons. He is only five years older than her and yet lately the gap, far from closing, has seemed to grow wider and wider. At forty-seven he was only that; at forty-eight he was already fifty; at forty-nine he was thinking of sixty: now, at fifty, he is seeing visions, behaving in a manner neither could explain. Still tender, honourable, distinguished, he is also still erotic — how else could this have happened? — but he is, too, a different person. His edges, once sharp, even elegant, have become softer, less visible, and unreliable in a way that nags at her but that she can not quite give words to. As if he is trying to betray her, without the slightest intention, in a way she can not fairly blame. The child, should a real child actually come, will be ten when he is sixty, but what age will he be then?

So it is that she is thinking as she stares vacantly at the vacant courtyard at a little after nine on a Thursday morning, reaching the last sentence, the last unnerving point of punctuation when

Mme Barber appears from the doorway opposite, one floor below. Mme Barber whom she thinks she once heard sobbing. Mme Barber and Catherine. The ground shifts. It is difficult to see the future, but sometimes the words for it yawn cavernously. She calls to Axel, wherever Axel is. By the time he answers it is already too late.

7

It is a large picture. Two pages. In it a mother is lying on her back on the ground with her three children. One of them, a girl, lies beside her in the very forefront. She looks as if she is about five or six years old. Another, younger child lies across the mother's legs while the third, a tiny baby wrapped in a tight bundle, lies on her chest. All of them are facing upward. It is winter. The mother and her older children are dressed in hats and scarves and tightly buttoned, double-breasted coats. The older children are staring at the sky and might be trying to make out shapes in the clouds. The mother and the baby have their eyes closed, and seem to be sleeping. But they are not, and the others are not watching the clouds. One of them — the one lying across the mother's legs, the one that Michael thinks is a boy — has a black mess where the left eye should be. The caption says only 'NAZI ATROCITIES IN THE UKRAINE' and then 'These are Russian peasants killed by the Germans in their retreat from Rostov-on-Don'.

Over the page there is a picture of the stern of a boat, its wake, and a great expanse of open sea. It is still winter. The men busy rolling off the depth charges are wearing heavy coats. On the right, on the opposite page, there is the crew of a German U-boat waiting nervously in the half-dark, looking up at the ceiling of the submarine as if in their minds' eyes they can see the other men above them. Michael holds up the page between the picture of the family and the picture of the sea — the page that has the dead boy on the one side and the ship's wake on the other — and looks closely at its edge, as if he has missed something and there were another page there that a gentle puff of his breath might reveal, a map, say, that showed how you got from one picture to the other, something he could hold in his own mind's eye. But there is nothing; only the strange way that the dead boy and the ocean disappear, leaving the young girl staring wide-eyed at the sky and the U-boat crew looking upward as if trying to see through the metal and the water above them, none of them able to see anything.

Michael puts the book down, turns off the bedside light and lies back, staring at the ceiling in the dark, trying to make his mind go blank, waiting for whatever those things are that seem to swim across the eyes like schools of tiny fish. Someone in the lane on the far side of the building places a heavy garbage bin on the stones. In the hallway his mother coughs and says something to his father. A shadow passes over the crack of light under the door. Sometime later he wakes in terror. He has been dreaming of running across a frozen lake with his mother and Thérèse. The men who have been chasing them have just caught up, are just about to grab hold of them. An arm is lying across his chest, a heavy weight, making it difficult to breathe. In horror he tries to throw it off, but it is difficult, since the arm is holding his own arm down, since his arm does not work. Somehow, at last, he moves it, only to find it is his own arm after all, a dead weight, that he has been sleeping on. Gradually, as his heart slows, as he tries to calm himself, the numbness goes, the feeling starts to come back.

8

Mme Lecault and Mme Berry continue to meet as before, but less and less frequently. Not for the first time it is as if a barrier that had slowly broken down has been rebuilt and is all the stronger and harder to surmount for the now certain knowledge of irremediable difference.

It may not be entirely that, however. Sometimes it seems to Mme Lecault as if she has caught a glimpse of a further, deeper sadness, as if something else, something ultimately far more disturbing has occurred. She gathers that others have come to the house — at least, Mme Berry now sometimes speaks of others — and that the demands upon her time and services are now much greater. But she will not elaborate, and no longer speaks even of the General. Instead she fends off questions even more nervously than she did in the early stages, attempting in turn to divert her friend with questions of her own. Even as these are answered, however, she listens only fitfully — as if, Mme Lecault has become convinced, she comes now less out of friendship than a need for distraction, or for some further, as yet undisclosable purpose, and finds it hard to keep her mind from whatever it is that troubles it.

The two have always relied upon a mutual insomnia to bring them together. This has generally been unpredictable, and there have been long periods when, as they have subsequently told each other, they have found themselves experiencing bouts of sleeplessness alone. They have fallen into a pattern, a rhythm, which each has learnt to endure patiently. But from the earliest stages neither would have said that they have actually tried to summon the other, nor, consciously, would they know how to do so if they wished. At a point some time after the first mention of others, however, this begins to change, and the relationship enters a further stage. In a way she would find hard to explain, it seems to Mme Lecault as if Mme Berry has begun to seek her out, to wait for her, to need her to come. For so long never appearing before two or three in the morning, she now does so earlier and earlier, chancing the possible encounters with the outside world. One night, Mme Lecault is convinced, she even contrives to be there already, waiting in the dark, on the chance that Mme Lecault, finding herself unable to sleep, might rise, and think of her, and walk into the room.

It is when, after some months of this, Mme Berry first asks her querulously where she has been, that Mme Lecault realises things have taken a significant new turn. Even then it is some time before she understands why.

9

Miklus then. All other possibilities she could as yet think of having been explored without success, Marguerite found herself returning again and again to his name. To all appearances he was healthy enough, it wasn't that, and his coming home drunk was hardly unusual; but perhaps she had misunderstood; perhaps she had been looking in the wrong direction, for the wrong kind of thing entirely. There were more kinds of distress than the physical, more kinds than would show themselves openly. Perhaps more kinds than the people who were causing or feeling them ever could know.

There was something, a moment, that she was trying to remember, that had passed almost before it had happened. Mme Lecault had mentioned some months ago that Miklus had wanted to talk to her about an alteration in their arrangements. She had been unable to go up to him on the day of the message, but had gone late the next morning and there had been no answer, nor on the next day when she had tried again. No further message having been left, she had thought it best to clean his apartment at her usual time on Thursday afternoon, and to leave it to him to contact her. Finding the key under the mat, she had let herself in and commenced work. The door to the studio had been closed, as always, and she had thought nothing of it: he had asked her, in any case, not to clean up in there. But when she had finished the bedroom and come in to start straightening and dusting the living room there had been a sound, a soft, brittle sound like the dropping of a pencil or paintbrush. She had stopped to listen, but there had been nothing further. Evidently he was in there working. She had continued her cleaning, but a thought had then struck her and she found herself increasingly uneasy. Perhaps she was not supposed to be there. Perhaps that had been the reason he had tried to get in touch with her. But perhaps, too, it was not the painter at all, and if it were not — if it were a thief instead — she would very likely receive the blame, since it would be evident that she had been there. Reluctantly then, but seeing no other option, she tapped at the door, wondering even as she did so whether she should have tapped harder. It opened slightly —

perhaps it had not been closed properly in the first place — and, hearing no answer, she tapped again, more boldly, and entered.

He stood there, in the middle of the room, a large figure in a golden-brown dressing-gown, staring at her with a wide-eyed look that she took at first for startled fury, but then realised — it was this realisation she was trying to recall — was possibly or also something else, like the strange vacancy of sleepwalkers who have been suddenly awakened and do not know where they are, or what they are looking at, or why. Behind him, in the corner lit by a large window, there was a girl sitting motionless, her eyes cast down, one arm up on the back of the chair and one breast exposed, a skirt pulled up high over her thighs. Catherine Barber. And the impression of fear. And then as quickly as it had arrived the moment had passed. Miklus was smiling and advancing toward her, apologising for the evident confusion, Catherine looking up brightly, smiling also as the door closed upon her. A cold hardness, a fleeting eeriness suddenly dissolved, leaving almost no traces.

Could it have been this? But what *was* this? Catherine had been posing for Miklus. Miklus worked in his robe. There had been no time to look at it but an easel had been there. And when he had gone back into the room, closing the door behind him, the painting had resumed. Since then nothing further had happened, nothing had changed. She had continued to clean the apartment on Thursdays, and on no occasion since had he been there; or, if he had, she had heard nothing (perhaps it had often been this way!). And if, that week, he had paid her a little extra, there was no reason to think anything in particular of it. All painters were like that. So why, now, did that moment come back? Why should she feel this greater need to know?

10

Somewhere a door is left open that has not been left open before. There is a change. A new note. Beneath or beyond the crying of the child, a set of different sounds. They are faint, barely distinguishable at first, but as the ear becomes accustomed, and since there are no other sounds but those of the infant, and one's own breath, one's heart, one does eventually hear them more clearly. The sounds of older people, parents perhaps, though they have never come before, and since the sounds of the infant are inexplicable enough there is no reason to think that these others come from the same place. Words, or it may not be words: the rising and falling, the coming and going of deeper tones. The sounds of people making love? Impossible, since the neighbours are the Professor and, on the far side of his apartment, the Countess, who is in any case away, or seems to be. But the sounds, the pattern, are familiar. Love-making, then, but also something more, a changing of the tone of some of the cries, as if, in the loving, there were also other elements — fear, aggression, brutality. A house within this house. And, further within, a great collapsing of the walls of the heart, as if glaciers calved.

Dreams, portents are also revisitations; revisitations are also portents. We cannot imagine using materials we do not have. Or can we? Isn't it also possible that, lacking them, the past — some lonely, some unspoken portion, broken away — wanders into the great, moonlit openness of the future, looking for someone who might tell it what it is?

11

At the first click of the key in the front door Michael closes the book, puts it on the floor under his bed, and turns off the bedside light. His mother comes in anyway, as he had hoped she would, and seems to know that he is awake. Perhaps they saw the light through his curtain as they came through the courtyard. If that was so she shows no sign of minding. She sits on the bed and reaches for him in the dark, and he allows himself to be pulled up — half sits up himself to make it easier — to receive the long, tight hug against the cool, stiff silk of her dress as she asks him what he has been doing and tells him a little about her night. He can hear the strong beating of her heart. He can smell wine on her breath, and around them both the heady scent of perfume — all through it, about it like a ring, a barricade, the smell of his father's cigars.

12

It has never been very easy between Tad and his mother. Maybe, if someone asked him, he might be able to remember vaguely a time when it was different, but for ages now there has been something wrong. Most of the time it is a vegetable. Most of the time it is a brussels sprout, a sprout that might have started out small enough, as brussels sprouts go, but that has grown somehow larger than any vegetable has ever any right to be, a brussels sprout as big as their life.

He can not eat vegetables. Carrots, cabbage, broccoli, beans, peas, spinach, turnip, onion, swede, pumpkin, squash, zucchini, aubergine, radish, celery, cauliflower, brussels sprout, it doesn't matter, although he might say especially brussels sprouts, and broccoli, and cauliflower, as if there could be degrees of the impossible. And it doesn't matter, either, whether you say that technically something isn't a vegetable but a fruit. Every time they force him to put part of one in his mouth he half vomits and it is all he can do to keep it there, to stop himself from spitting it out onto the table. She knows that, and so does his father, and they know too that if they do force him to swallow — that if he could manage it, past the part of him that is wanting to gag on it, and while everything is becoming blurry with the tears and the rage — that by the next day he will have the white rash anyhow, on his legs or his arms or his neck or belly, and that there is nothing he can do to stop it.

Doctor Maurois a long time ago told them that it is all in his mind, and that it was time they helped him get over it, and ever since then they have pushed him. His mother really, since his father always tries to stay out of it and only says something when she demands that he does so. First of all it was just that she would put something on his plate — a bit of carrot, say, or some cauliflower — and let him make up his own mind about it. But that never worked. The juice from the vegetable would seep over onto his chop or his mashed potato — he *can* eat potato — and make it taste metallic and awful, so that he even had trouble eating that. Then she started hiding small bits of things in his mashed potato, so that it got so he daren't touch it just in case. And then they started trying to force him. It wasn't that they actually put some vegetable in his mouth and made him swallow, but they wouldn't let him have any dessert until he had tasted a bit of pumpkin, or eaten a pea or two, and then, when he had gone without dessert for too long, they started to keep him at the table. Everyone else would have finished dinner and dessert and everything, and he had to keep on sitting there, not allowed to get up until he had eaten whatever it was that they gave him — some beans, some spinach, a small piece of watery turnip. They didn't do this every night; his mother said that she couldn't stand it; but every now and then, once or twice every week or so. Sometimes it seemed to him that it was most likely to happen when his mother was angry about something else. It was almost as if she *chose* to make everything worse, because he was sure she knew just as well as he did that there was nothing he could do about it.

And then, at last, there was the brussels sprout, and that has been more or less an end to it. There had been veal, and chips, and brussels sprouts, which were his father's favourite. She put one, a big one, on his plate, and all through the meal she watched him try to eat around it and grew angrier and angrier. Her face got redder, and there was less and less talk, and the room seemed to get smaller and tighter and hotter about them. He ate the meat and the chips, and left the sprout sitting there. No one said anything, but when she brought the dessert out, and everyone else had been served, he wasn't given any. Still no one said anything. Then, when Mara and his father left the table, and she wanted to clear the dishes away, she transferred the brussels sprout to a bread and butter plate, one of the white ones with the thick blue line around the rim, and left him sitting there. Something different was happening, but he wasn't sure what. After she did the dishes she came back and sat down at the table facing him. In a low, steady, furious voice she said that he was going to sit there until he ate it, as long as ever it took, that she was fed up and this was the last straw. She went off and put Mara to bed, and then sat for a while with his father in the lounge room, listening to the radio. Then everything was quiet, everything calmed down for a while.

When she came back she was carrying his father's belt, folded over as if she was going to hit him with it. She stood for a long while beside the chair. Once or twice she tapped the belt against her leg, but most of the time she just stood there. She seemed huge right then, a sort of living oven or furnace, a volcano. Maybe she was going to hit him, and maybe not. It didn't seem to matter. He was tired and had gone blank somehow. The brussels sprout had long gone cold. It looked sad and shabby on the white surface, darker and slightly shrunken. Around the base, still stuck to it, was a burred frill of congealed grease that had broken away when it had been moved from the first plate to the second.

Eventually she went away. Once or twice he heard noises from the other room or muffled sounds from the courtyard, but mostly there was only a kind of distant hum behind things, and eventually a softer sound, like a long, steady wind in a tree far off somewhere. His mind wandered and came back, and wandered away again. Sometimes it seemed as if he had been a long way from the table and he was surprised when he found himself back there again. No one came for him. At last, when he was sure that he had been falling asleep and waking at his chair, he got up and was going to ask if he might be allowed to go to bed, but only the reading lamp in the lounge room was on and everyone was already asleep. It was just after two in the morning. When he woke up the plate was gone, and although for most of the day his mother didn't speak to him, that had soon changed. Since then no one has tried to get him to eat vegetables. It seems as if things are all right between his mother and him, but this isn't really so. Somewhere about them there is always the ghost of a huge, cold brussels sprout, that rotted away long ago, but the stink of which still lingers, even if only on the poorly wiped, damp-surfaced table in their minds.

13

It is late afternoon on a Friday, the Professor's market day, and he returns from his shopping carrying a basket more heavily laden than usual. He pats this significantly, with a conspiratorial smile, as he passes Mme Lecault at her kitchen window, but, the question to which this is in fact a good-humoured, teasing response having been asked some months earlier, she can only shrug bemusedly and turn again to peeling her potatoes. Tonight is M. Christophe's meeting night, and as usual she will feed Thérèse and Stéphane. The few extra francs each week help her — every little bit does — but she would do it anyway: has been doing it, one way or another, for years.

In the Professor's basket — how could she know it? — are a large, bright orange pumpkin and a fat rooster, freshly killed. There are also some sweet purple onions, some potatoes, two large peppers (*anchos*), one green and one yellow, and almost a kilo of smaller red peppers of the kind they call *chipotle*. The Professor has gone to considerable trouble to find the correct peppers, and has actually had to order the *chipotle* especially, but the best things take time. A further ingredient has also proved difficult to track down. It is the promise, at last, from a Spanish butcher in the worker's quarter, that it can be ready for him the Friday following, that has sent him now into action. The timing has been carefully planned. It should take him just under a week to get the rest ready. The only other things he needs — thyme, parsley, tarragon, garlic — will come fresh from Auguste's garden.

14

April 1945: on the 1st the U.S. 1st Army clears Paderborn and enters Hamm; on the 8th the Russians launch an attack on Königsberg; on the 12th Roosevelt dies and Mr Truman is sworn in as President; on the 15th the Allied armies, on their eastern flank, reach the Elbe on their push towards Berlin, and in the north push closer and closer to Hamburg. There is a photograph of British tanks on the road from Celle to Bergen. In one of the armoured cars behind them — it is impossible to tell which — is Captain Derek Sington, in command of No. 14 Amplifying Unit of the 11th Armoured Division. Soon, in that eerie emptiness between one page and the next, the column of which he is a part will reach the village of Bergen itself. Soon, arriving at the gate of a large encampment, he will step out and walk towards the man he will later introduce to Brigadier Glyn Hughes as Josef Kramer. Already small clusters of emaciated inmates are gathering at the high fences. People already know and yet do not know. People are already bracing themselves.

15

Saturday, bright Saturday. Jean-Luc Bloch has risen early and gone out to the library, leaving his wife in bed with coffee and a fresh brioche. Michael, on the other hand, sleeps on (she does not want to wake him), rising eventually in the late morning, at which time she makes him an omelette — chopping chives, parsley and a touch of tarragon into it as he has always liked — and herself another cup of coffee to sip while he eats. He seems a little strange this morning, soft and affectionate but also nervous. Later, when he has dressed and gone out to visit a friend on rue Riviére, she discovers the reason, or what might be the reason. Having showered, dressed, cleaned away the few breakfast dishes, she prepares to do the week's washing and, stripping Michael's bed, finds a cold, stiffening patch of semen on the bottom sheet. This is the third time, at least, that this has happened, and she knows that it should not disturb her — Jean-Luc has told her that boys have such dreams, that it need not be the sign of anything else — but for some reason today it does. The washing done she finds herself restless, impatiently awaiting the return of Jean-Luc or Michael, unable to decide whether to go out or stay at home — to listen to music perhaps — trying to calm herself.

Eventually the weather decides the matter for her. What began with warm sunshine turns colder, becomes overcast, threatening rain. Her restlessness in its own turn gives way at first to a vaguer anxiety, then to a growing sadness. Trying to read she finds herself instead staring into the middle distance, a welter of ancient memories flooding her consciousness: grey days by a fire in her grandparents' chateau; Jean-Luc when she had first met him, fixing his bicycle in the rain; the fights with her mother over him; the hot, damp smell of her mother's apron; the smell of her father;

the smell, the taste of someone else, in the orangery, earlier, before everything had come to change her — before the war, in the time she hardly dared to remember. Coming back to herself she finds the cold suddenly upon her, entering her bones, and rises, shuddering, drawing her cardigan about her. Taking her book, she goes to her bed where — the curtains drawn and her clothes removed, blankets pulled high against the cold and her eyes closed, her cold hands between her thighs for warmth — something else begins and takes hold of her, is guided by her, in widening, concentric circles, rhythmic movements, a dream of red and orange, warm greens and blacks, not rainbows but something slower, earth-bows, blood-bows, ending at last in a sobbing that seems to have come from nowhere, everywhere, the one forgotten syllable — or perhaps it is two of them, almost a name — drawn through her again and again, like a heavy chain slowly through the hand. And Jean-Luc, somehow, Jean-Luc, who has come in after all, and found her naked, and now only gently weeping, and thinks that something is wrong. Naked and gently weeping, her hands hot and still trembling, smelling strangely of oranges.

16

The door pushes open easily — it seems it never does close properly — and reveals the same bare room she remembers from her earlier glimpses, the sunshine flooding in from the corner window, the uncovered boards, canvases leaning against the inner wall arranged in their sizes, their faces turned away from the light. There is a second window she hasn't seen before; it would have been obscured by the door; and before it a small, cluttered table, leaning against the wall to the right of which is a single large painting, its face likewise turned from the sun.

The pictures — it is these, after all, that she has come to see — are of various subjects: a bowl of a fruit so bright and red that in the heat of them she has to think for a moment to realise that they are cherries; a still life of a ruler, vases, paper, brushes and a coffeepot on a table, *that* table, with the stacked paintings evident behind it; a half-finished portrait of Catherine Barber asleep with her head on the card table usually kept in the cupboard in the hallway, and then, here, larger, the painting she has hoped to find: Catherine, sitting in the chair, just as she had been on the day she had interrupted them, one breast exposed, the black skirt drawn up high on her thigh, but unexpectedly alone, wistful, as if Miklus had never been there, as if nobody was there at all, and the effect not of fear — why had she expected it? — but of softness, of gentleness, of warm, ambered light.

It troubles her back to stoop at this angle, and yet she dares not move the paintings too far from their place lest he see that someone has touched them. Taking the chair from the drawing-strewn table she sits down beside them, able now to lean them one by one against her right knee. There is also a half-finished study of the rooftops outside, with cats and pigeons, one or two of them blurred in flight; there is a study of someone who might have been Thérèse Christophe (the face is slightly obscured), lying back in one of the armchairs from the other room, gazing vacantly into the middle distance; there is a portrait of M. Bernard sitting in the same chair in which Catherine was sitting, leaning forward, his elbows on his knees, staring straight out with a startled, owlish look, as if someone had just said something very strange to him or he were embarrassed to be found like this; there is a portrait of Lucien Christophe, in a suit, seated with his arms around a Stéphane and a Thérèse much younger than they are now; there is a painting of the lemon tree in the courtyard with her own kitchen window just visible behind it, the top of her vinegar jar protruding above the sill, and the rim of the soapdish she always keeps there, her old curtains — the curtains she only recently replaced — tied back in their tired bows. (When did he do this? It can't have been long ago. Mme Maurois only gave her the jar last Christmas. And yes, it's true, the lemons were particularly beautiful this year, huge, glowing globes in the dark leaves, that shone as if by their own light, right up until midnight or after.) Then — the second-last painting, smaller than the rest, and out of sequence, since they seem to be arranged by size — a simple picture of what at first she thinks are fat and foreshortened irises, just opening, but then realises with pleasure are no more than stalks of asparagus in a white milk jug.

To see the largest painting, closest to the wall, she has to move the others and lean them against the door. This done she pulls it back and is lucky not to drop it in her fright. Uneasy lest Miklus should return suddenly and discover her, but unable to stop herself, and scarcely believing what she sees, she turns it carefully, wheeling it on its bottom corner until it leans face-forward to the light. It is Catherine again, but this time naked, lying stretched out on the same armchair, her eyes closed, her arms flung back, her legs slightly apart as if she has fainted in abandon. All about her the shadows of the room are dark and the light from the window — the same window that is now shedding a golden, late-afternoon light on the picture itself — is somehow hard, obtrusive, threatening.

In the sudden chill the painting seems to have introduced —

is it sudden, or has she been standing there for an age? — she becomes again conscious of time and place. Carefully she re-stacks the paintings as she found them, her curiosity all but evaporated. Whatever arrangements M. Miklus makes with the children and the parents of the house are their own affair. Whether she has found what she expected to or otherwise would be difficult to say, and the question has in any case gone from her mind. The light has grown rapidly colder. She has wasted too much time here already.

Placing the chair back at the table, however, she notices again the drawings on it and remembers the one large canvas leaning against the wall beside it. Almost without thinking she turns its face toward her and is taken aback by the blue. The pervasive, colour-engulfing blue of pre-dawn and the last of dusk, or of summer, lemon-tree nights when the moon is lowest and most full and there is an utterly cloudless sky. It is a street scene, at the corner of rue Rivière and rue Thélin, hardly a block from the house, but a scene that could surely never actually have been. Michael Bloch, wide-eyed in the foreground, seems about to stumble directly into the painter, while behind him are Mme Lecault — at the intersection, moving up rue Thélin, carrying a bag as if she were shopping (at that hour?) — and just behind her, disappearing along rue Rivière, a man carrying what at first seems the end of a coffin, though on second thought it is more probably the end of a long, wide plank. And in the middle ground, in the short, cobblestoned stretch between Michael and the intersection, sitting in the gutter or standing idly on the pavements, lost in thought, or as if they have simply come out late at night to bathe in what would have to be the strongest moonlight of the year, the Professor, Mme Barber, Auguste, Lucien Christophe,

Catherine, Ivan, Tad. Moonstruck, all of them; moonstruck, and not really themselves.

Somewhere far off, a whole room away, a key turns in a lock.

17

They have gone! Vanished! Disappeared without trace. Paul and Justine — the Lovers, the Couple-With-The-Name-Like-The-Sky. Mme Lecault cannot say when or why. She is livid, furious, as much with herself as with the apparent offenders. And deeply embarrassed. All the more so because there is no one else she could possibly blame. She had left them alone. That is the way they had wanted it. And repeatedly extended them credit. Now, as she calculates it, they owe her for almost two months, and she can think of no way whatever to recover the loss. She might not even have known now had it not been for the need to inform everyone that the water would be cut off all day Tuesday. Most of them she could rely upon to see the notice outside her door, but she had suddenly remembered the Lovers, and realised that she had not seen either of them for over two weeks — that she had better go up herself, to make sure they knew.

No one answered, nor when she went back the next day. She had become concerned and returned on the third with the master key. The heavy curtains were almost fully closed, as Paul and Justine had always kept them — that is what had fooled her — and when she opened them it was to find nothing, or at least nothing that had not been there already before they moved in: nothing but that earth smell, that strange, fresh, winter smell they brought with them when they came.

18

The Professor likes to work steadily during the day, and it is not until early evening that he allows himself any of the rituals he now holds so sacred: the peeling of vegetables, the chopping of herbs, the preparation, when his diet allows, of white or pink or deep-red flesh, the long and careful consideration beforehand of the perfect wine, whether or not he eventually chooses to open it. Tonight, while the rooster simmers in an iron pot, he prepares a large salad of spinach leaves, mushrooms and tomato, tossed with diced bacon, black pepper, a finely chopped egg and a light dressing of oil and lemon juice, enjoying as he does so the scents, the textures, the meetings of knife-blade and wood no less than he will the meal itself, eaten from a white china plate upon a fresh linen tablecloth beside a three-pronged candelabra and a half-loaf of the coarse brown bread made by Mme Lacoste, the entire apartment — as, he imagines quite correctly, the courtyard beyond it — filled with the rich, yellow pungency of fowl.

Reflecting that this, being the eve of his sixty-seventh birthday, could be construed as a special occasion, he has opened a bottle of sweet, crisp white wine the name of which translates as the Tears of Christ. Domenico Scarlatti is playing on the turntable. When the high, lonely tumult of the harpsichord is finished, his mind alive with swallows and clear mountain streams, the Professor takes the white wine and a glass to his desk, and begins to write to his friend in South America.

Dear Paulo,

Thank you a thousand times for the recipe! I am sorry to have taken so long to answer, but so many things have happened to delay me, and the punishment in any case is mine, since it's already long past Easter and the soup will now have to be a spring, not an autumn feast.

After some trouble with the ingredients I have at last commenced and hope within the week to sit down to the soup of soups. I am only sorry that it is not you who will be making it for me, as once in Saint Girond, and that we will not be sitting down to it together. But I am used to dining with ghosts — there is rarely anyone else — and can be sure that in that sense I will not dine alone.

Mostly I thank you for writing so warmly and so generously. I am sorry to have said so little in my own first letter to deserve it, but not knowing who would read my words I thought it best, until I had confirmed your whereabouts, to use as few as possible. And speech, after twenty years of silence, is surely difficult, for anyone.

No, I am not particularly happy, or have not been (what a question!), and not always well. Having descended so much into the flesh it seems I must now live or not live as the flesh directs. But you will remember that I always complain, and I trust will take it accordingly.

I am no longer at the university, but resigned them my professorship two years ago. It was not comfortable. My old loves came here with me, if only as rumours, sounds in seashells, and it seems at last became too much for one or two ambitious colleagues. There was whispering in corridors, and what I had never tried to bury was suddenly unearthed, to a convenient, familiar, and doubtless carefully orchestrated horror. When all that had stopped long ago and for years my greatest indulgence — I will not say my only — has been opera!

Now, at last, after these same twenty years, I am writing on the plays of Shakespeare. An Italian professor, living in France, writing about an Englishman. When you think that so much of what that Englishman wrote was about the French, the Italians, there is perhaps some justice to it, but of course it is another Shakespeare I am writing of . . .

My book on Villon has been translated into English and Spanish, and is now again available here, through a reprint company in Paris. I am told — or used to be — that I am famous in a small way: no one can write about him who has not read my work. I am sure that that too made them uncomfortable, my petty and ambitious colleagues: the overweight, alcoholic homosexual ex-priest who could not control his bitter tongue, was also a successful scholar! (and a better one than they).

You will throw up your hands — I was always on your hands — and pray for me, but we are each moving in our separate ways and if geography is any metaphor we may therefore meet yet, you via the soul's eye, me, with any luck (ah! what a dream!) through the sweet, tight arsehole of a boy.

I do hope we meet. I might almost pray for it. Life has already offered us less likely things.

In sincere friendship and affection,

Giovanni.

P.S. Tonight I drank a bottle of Lacryma Christi. One of the labels — it was a Mastroberardino — tells a story I must have heard as a child, but had long since forgotten. Do you remember it? When God threw Satan out of Heaven a small portion of Paradise fell out with him and became the Bay of Naples. God cried long and bitterly, and the tears fell to earth on the slopes of Vesuvius where the vineyards lie, so giving to their wine that distinctive character that some have called unearthly. (And bequeathing also, presumably, some curly questions concerning human existence (particularly for Neapolitans), viz., are we on earth, in heaven, or in hell, or is it that we are in all three simultaneously? (And is it unearthly, or is it merely — and no less exquisitely — of broom and elderflowers? (I think I am drunk, dear Paulo. So much I get for writing on an empty stomach! Good night. Wish me luck for the Soup.)))

An hour, two hours pass, much of them spent staring into nothingness. The swallows depart. The streams run to large, sluggish estuaries. At last, the short letter long finished — it is only a short letter after all — he turns off the low flame beneath the iron pot, then strains the stock into a large stoneware bowl and covers it with a cloth. The wine has lost its chill. With what is left of it he eats the salad and all of the bread, wiping the plate and the salad bowl with the crusts of it, amazed at how hungry he is, how delicious, tonight, every morsel has been.

The table cleared and the plates washed, he resists the temptation to open a second bottle — this time of the rich, heavy Rhône the doctor tells him will poison him — and pours himself instead a small glass of Benedictine, the honey, the brandy, the myrrh on his tongue performing a more benign if perhaps also darker magic, under the spell of which he plays the mournful concerto by Bruch, sitting long into the silence afterward, remembering the distant and the recent dead — for those who betray us are also departed — retiring to bed only when he hears, from almost a mile away, the town clock strike two. By the time he rises in the morning the stock will have become a strong, clear jelly, and there will have formed on its surface a thin layer of fat. This he will remove and, having melted the large white disk in a skillet, mix with scraps from the rooster-bones (the rest he will save for a vol-au-vent) and place in the courtyard for the cats.

19

A garden is not always what you intend — Auguste is trying to explain something to Michael, who has just asked about the number of tomato shoots growing amongst the early flowers, away from the kitchen plot — the more you know about gardening the more you are tempted to let things take their own course.

At Michael's apparent surprise he qualifies this. It can go the other way, of course — in fact it usually does — but it is the way he, Auguste, feels.

It began toward the end of the war. He had been away: not fighting. No, bugger them! In any case the army would not let him because of his eye; but the Germans had taken him in and sent him to a camp near Nice. They had intended to send him further, out of the country, but the retreat had come first. When he got back — it had been over a month — the whole herb garden, eight foot by six, had been taken over by basil. He'd never seen it so green or so healthy, or known it to smell so wonderfully. He had wanted to throw himself down in it, after so much anxiety, and roll around and drown in the huge and luxurious scent of it. You had never seen leaves so large and green, so rich and fat and heavy with oil. Maybe it was an omen, the garden's celebration of the going of the lousy, arrogant Germans, but also maybe not: surely something — surely herbs — shouldn't have to know of such things. Ever since, anyway, he'd let them do what they wanted: the basil, the dill, and anything else that had wanted to stray. Three or four times in the last ten years the same thing had happened and there'd been more basil than he could give away. Plants have laws of their own. Parsley, for example, that is supposed to grow best in the gardens of the wicked: he'd never had any trouble growing parsley, though for the life of him he couldn't see how he'd managed the wickedness, willing and able enough as he was. Perhaps the thoughts alone could do it; in which case, well . . .

The dill had been similar. One year — it was 1951 or '52 —

he'd been so busy with new plots at the river end that it had all gone to seed before he noticed. By the time he'd got to them he'd found the dill stalks dry and fallen on the ground. In his annoyance he'd gathered them and burnt them, and hadn't thought about the seeds. He'd dug the plot over and planted aubergines (they'd done well too: there is no vegetable so beautiful to look at or hold), but ever since, each year, the plot had been laced with tiny, feathery shoots of dill. Nothing he did seemed to get rid of them, and eventually he'd stopped trying. Like the pumpkin flowers. You never put pumpkin seeds in the compost. But whoever said that had forgotten about the flowers. He'd rather have them there than not. Ever since the day he'd heard about the death of M. Gandhi — about how they were going to cremate him — and first noticed the bright orange cannons of a pumpkin vine rising from the back of the compost, like flames.

And so the tomatoes — he finally gets to the tomatoes. 'A couple of years ago', he tells Michael — they have been walking all around the garden looking for aphids, and have just come back to the plot in question — 'I sowed the small, climbing kind, the kind you need frames for. The bushes got through the chicken wire and started to fruit where I couldn't pick it. I couldn't tear them down until the rest had finished, and so when I got around to it there were little tomatoes rotting all over the ground. I scraped up what I could, and then last year I broke up the bed. It was good, rich soil — dozens of worms to the spadeful; the ground was alive with them, squirming and popping up everywhere — and I used it all over the garden. Now there are tomato plants all over the place, even in the irises. Certainly no one will stop them if I don't, and I'm not going to. This year the whole house will have tomatoes.'

20

The Countess, too, has not been seen for some time. The signs are there, for any who might care to notice them — the mail collected from her pigeonhole, slight changes in the arrangement of the closed curtains at her windows, the late night sounds, for those only a wall away, of a chair moving, running water; there is even, should anyone be so prurient as to inspect, her garbage bin, with all the usual litter and an even greater than normal proportion of empty packets of Gitanes, discarded writing paper — but few, if they were asked, could say for certain when it was that they last saw her, or what it was that she was doing, what she was carrying, whom it was who might have accompanied her. Whether, say, the tall, dark-haired young man she has sometimes been seen with — the man with the exhausted eyes — or whether she had seemed depressed or preoccupied, whether it was a book she was holding, or a package, an umbrella, a basket of food, or what it might have been that she was wearing.

21

In the soft light, the half-focus, the tangle of arms and legs, it is hard, but for a few very obvious exceptions, to tell age or gender. Male is becoming female, the trunks and limbs of the young attached to the heads of the old, the bodies of the old, already younger in their nakedness, given the faces of the beautiful innocent. Here the genitals are openly, flagrantly exposed — a penis like a small white grub, a tiny apostrophe of light; a woman's sex, between her widespread knees, like an hourglass of darkness — but to which face they belong, which head thrown back, which arm or finger pointing as if casually toward which other, can't be made out. Here one's attention is caught by the furrows of a rib cage, the calibrations of a spine, there by the glint of light off a femur, the anomaly of a fragment of cloth in this welter of nakedness. Everywhere there is abandon, the softness of deepest exhaustion. One woman, on the edge of the group, lies like a gazelle, long limbs that might normally gangle or trudge now stretched out in infinite gentleness and grace. Others lie as if, running, they have flung themselves headlong into the shallow space, or dived there, or fallen tumbling, still others as if they were swimming somehow, or burrowing, or worming through. One figure, in the background, is hunched, scrabbling for something in the dirt, as if she has lost a ring, a coin; another, in the foreground, seems caught, still deeply sleeping, at the moment of turning in her bed; another, in a momentary clearing in the sea of limbs, lies with her head and arms thrown back and torso arched, her mouth and eyes wide open in what, away from here, could almost be ecstasy.

You can *see* something, but to say, even to yourself alone, that you *have* seen it is to do something to it, to begin to bring it further into being, to begin to come closer to knowing the being that it has. Not simply to say 'yes, I see it; I do see that', but to name it, to call its parts by the words they are known by, to say 'I see the black woman with a cherry on her head', or 'I see the man still in his prison tunic, pinned to the side of the trench, his pants off and his arms flung out as if the grey sky were about to swallow him'. To say this, then; but to say it *aloud*, to *tell*, is to go further, and to write it down, to try to preserve one's words, is to try to go further still, not merely for the keeping that it must also be, but for the work of the muscles around the idea's shape, for the calling of the body to the fashioning of signs. And then, for there is a further still, an even greater coming-into-being than this, to find the place of that writing in something wider.

But there are things that are outside words, that words can crash upon, over and over, and endlessly fall away.

These things, some of them, occur to Michael as he gazes. But also something else, something the opposite of these. After a time it seems to him as if, in his mind, he has been moving slowly over the tangle of bodies attaching here and there a label — 'hand', 'arm', 'mouth', 'gazelle' — and that the labels have been crumbling, blowing away even as he does so. Soon it is the eyes only, moving repeatedly back and forth. But even these, repelled by the light off limbs, off torsos, off faces, the miniscule cracks of light between the grains of which such photographs are composed, cannot penetrate the darkness behind them.

22

A man has been coming to see the Countess for two or three weeks now. It would be hard to determine exactly how often. Mme Lecault has seen him on four or five occasions and it is rather unlikely, vigilant as she is, that there have been many more. Miklus has seen him once or twice, as has Thérèse. He is a man of a little over average height, though not very much more, and of distinguished appearance, his beard neatly trimmed in the manner of Louis Napoleon, his hair — what one can see of it beneath the dark hat — peppered with grey. Always wearing a coat. Always, as is only reasonable, given the recent rains, carrying an umbrella. And always, apparently, quite without luck. On most occasions Mme Lecault is quite sure that this has been because the Countess was not at home, though at least once she could have sworn otherwise. It is not her business to pry. If people wish to leave messages with her then that is always possible. If they choose not then that too is their affair. But it is very tempting — so elegant and so interesting as he seems — to call out to him as he passes, to see whether she might help. So elegant and so interesting, and also something else, a harmlessness or defencelessness, that stimulates sympathy. The way he knocks only once, and not loudly, then stands waiting just a little longer than another might, though less from impatience — he seems very patient indeed — or from the urgency of his mission than from a kind of puzzlement, as if, having visited only in dreams, he can not be sure that this is the right place but also can not think of another, or as if the thick wooden door itself were some curiously animate thing, able to assess him of its own accord.

23

Mme Berry has begun to conduct experiments. She starts to bring things with her. At first of the smallest kind — a bejewelled thimble, a tiny mirror, a coffee cup of the finest china — but then increasingly larger: a book of recipes, a vase. In each case there is some pretext — she had spoken of the item, perhaps, and Mme Lecault had expressed a wish to see it — but there seems also to be a pattern, an idea or theory being tested. At one point she brings a large bouquet of herbs — fresh tansy, woodruff, burnet, winter savory, lovage — and insists that Mme Lecault keep it and use all she can. It is, Mme Lecault thinks, with a disproportionate excitement, almost relief, that Mme Berry hears, when next she comes, that her friend has used a substantial portion and has carefully dried the rest. She insists on being told as much as she can about the dishes to which they were added, the tastes and effects they produced, and when Mme Lecault brings out some of the dried stems to show her she fingers them with evident delight.

Delight, however, does not hide the underlying tension, nor entirely free Mme Berry from whatever it is that distracts her. Despite her clear pleasure at the use of the herbs, Mme Lecault senses, from the frequency with which they are now mentioned, that the others of whom her friend had earlier spoken are now a source of particular anxiety. With a receptive look, an expectant silence, she offers Mme Berry more than once the opportunity to confide — what possible harm could come of transporting her troubles into another century? — but a by-now familiar reticence, a change of subject each time answers her, and she understands yet again that there are inhibitions and superstitions she may never understand.

It shocks her then, and throws her into a flurry of subsequent speculations, when, just as she is leaving — just as she is about to vanish through the solid wall — Mme Berry turns and tells her, clearly, urgently, more forcefully than she has ever yet spoken, that next time, if it can be done — if God will allow it; if He will help her (this God who knows no time, this God who is eternal) — she will bring someone with her. Pausing only a moment in her astonishment, Mme Lecault finds none the less that she has addressed her next and perhaps all too obvious question to a blank wall.

24

The rue des Girondins has never been so wide or so crowded. She has been sent by her father to buy something from a greengrocery, several things, apples, pears, aubergines, large, overripe tomatoes, a large, perfect peach. Leaving the shop she walks to the corner — *they* walk, since now there is another with her, a woman, holding her hand, making it harder to carry the basket — hearing shouts, and the sounds of people running, louder and louder. It's an overcast day, the kind of light she saw once when there was an eclipse, like a summer dusk at midday when the shadow of the moon goes over the sun, and then, suddenly, there is the crowd again, and they are caught in it, struggling against it, even though she knows that what is behind, causing the people to run, is going to be something terrible. There is another sound, a sort of dull clattering that began in short bursts and is now almost continuous. Suddenly the crowd breaks and there is the wide open street, empty of anything but blood, a trickle at first that soon becomes a stream, a river, flowing toward her along the gutter, pushing against her, making it harder to walk (or is it the woman, who is now on the ground, whose hand is now strangely on her ankle?) — the blood, bright red and shining like velvet, and things shooting past her in the air. And then a sudden pain, a throbbing at the pit of her stomach. Dropping her hands to the place, spilling the basket out onto the street, the fruit and the vegetables; blood, and, waking, a wetness she has never felt before. Although, placing her hand there, feeling for it, she knows already what it is.

25

It is late Thursday afternoon. Perplexed over a passage in *Richard the Third*, the Professor has come down from his study and sliced the pumpkin, cutting it into quarters and then halving the pieces again before starting to pare off the thick orange rind. Cutting the pieces again into halves he simmers them with lightly browned onion in the rooster-broth, adding a little salt and a small, dried chili. He then halves the smaller peppers and gently steams them before placing them in a dish in the refrigerator. They must be limp, he remembers, and velvet to the touch, and a bright scarlet, like the petals of a giant, fleshy tulip.

When the pumpkin is ready he separates it from the broth and mashes it, returning as much of the broth as is needed to produce a thick, golden soup. The halved *chipotles* and the larger *anchos*, carefully roasted until they are semidried, he will not add until an hour before serving a few nights hence, at the same time as for additional colour he stirs in thick chunks of a large beefsteak tomato straight out of Auguste's garden.

Tomorrow he will go to the markets for his usual weekly supplies, and then across the river for the six blood-red combs. These he will pound with coarse-ground black pepper, slice lengthwise with his sharpest knife, and stir in to marinate amongst the *chipotle*. He will separate them again, before the peppers go in, and add them only minutes before serving. *Cock soup*, he thinks again, as if running over a familiar litany, *the soup of generals, dictators, conquistadors*, but also, in celebration, of those who have suffered, of those who have chased them away.

26

There was no time to lose. He wakes with the words spilling out of him, remarkable words, and now there is no time to lose. He has been talking with someone, and they have given it to him, an explanation, an ultimate answer, and now, awake, the words are still there, still forming their magical sentences, their elegant, necessary simplicities. He knows that he could get up, could go to the study to write them down, but there is not the time, he dares not risk losing them out there in the darkness — he can feel them, they might almost be in his hand, like the rarest delicate dried flower, a bird's bones in sand — in the search for paper, for pencil, and the risk of waking Hélène, having to speak, explain, when here on the sidetable are the materials he needs, the novel he is reading, that he remembers has two or three blank leaves inside the back cover, and one of the new ballpoint pens Benoit left for him. Bedclothes partly thrown back, the book open on the mattress beside him, his fingers telling him the top and edge of the page, he begins to write, to get it all down, anything, everything he can remember, in whatever shape or order it comes, not lingering — already they are crumbling! — for the exact word or phrase, knowing there will be time enough in daylight to sort out such things, such extraordinary things, the path of the thought so clear, so simple before him, like the true nature, the true purpose of being, *his* being, the pen's tip slipping over the page's edge, guided back by the right hand, no true sense of the shape of letters, the direction of a line, knowing that if only the faintest trace is recorded, the most garbled form of a word or a letter, he will somehow, in daylight, remember, recall, restore it.

And yet of course it is not that way. In daylight, waking again, he turns immediately to the table, burning to see the book and the things he has written, only to find that the pen has not worked, has left only — so quickly had he written — the slightest, most useless indentations, and, once or twice, since once or twice the ink had sputtered, the saddest abandoned serif. There is nothing,

nothing, and the words — try as he might to remember, to rescue them, to summon even their merest ghosts by rubbing a pencil over them — are gone. His dismay at first is almost desperate, and yet it calms, eventually, and the subsequent depression passes. He comes even to think that it is perhaps better this way. Such knowledge — for he is sure that that is what it was — would almost certainly be difficult to live with, to contain, and yet to know that there has been — there *is* — such a clarity of path, such vision, keeps him, reassures him somehow, about a great deal else.

27

There has been a smell, a rotting smell, a smell of death and decay, faintly but distinctly foul, though whether of animal or vegetable is difficult to say. Not exactly all-pervasive, in fact far from from it, a furtive smell, a hit-and-run smell, a guerilla, skulking about the bins and drains, lying in wait in exhaust vents, pockets of stagnant air, the corners of long-closed rooms. It ambushes Jean-Luc Bloch as he takes out his garbage one Sunday evening; it assails Catherine Barber as she sweeps the tiny hallway of the three-room apartment; it keeps Hélène Ségur awake one night despite the fact that Axel can smell nothing at all; it dogs Mme Pizac and causes Auguste more than once to shudder and move off swiftly when he encounters it lying like an invisible pool amongst the irises.

And yet it is also — how can one put this? — as if it is no smell at all; a rumour, a fleeting evanescence, rather than the thing itself. Those who might think they have caught it — who think that they might at last have remembered what it was (for it is often also hauntingly familiar) — step back to where it had seemed they passed through it only to find it gone, as often as not replaced by something else they could not possibly have mistaken for it, something sweeter, an icy fragrance, as if it were also a parasite smell, a smell beneath a smell, or these other more pleasant smells were revealing a darker side that they had never before disclosed.

There are complaints, of course, but what can be done? Sympathetic as Mme Lecault might be (how could it be otherwise, since she has been assailed as often as any?), she is no bloodhound, and there is a clear limit to the time she can spend chasing something so sporadic and elusive. When at last an afternoon is given over, with Auguste, and with Mara Pizac as ferret, no explanation is found, not even the smell itself.

Explanations vary. The most common is that some thing has died somewhere within the baffling interstices of the building — or rather things, since only a plurality of small and random decompositions could explain the scattered nature of the phenomenon — and that the tiny air-currents and passageways with which those interstices abound carry the smell to sites far from its source or sources. Others believe it an indication that the plumbing and the drains are in need of thorough overhaul. Still others speculate that it is not a thing of this building at all, but a smell from next door or across the street, carried in on one of the intermittent freak breezes that worm their way down into the narrow streets and alleys and laneways of the quarter. Does anyone know? No, of course not. Nobody knows. Still another possibility is that it is not *a* smell at all, but several, for how could any two people compare accurately something so very nearly ineffable? Or that it is not even smells, but Smell, and that there are very few times at all in the history of a place such as this when such a thing has not been around, for weeks, months, years, in some form or another.

28

The night has corridors. The talk runs long into the dark, the many hours between two and three, or three and four unknown to those who have not strayed sleepless past hidden entrances and felt the draught, or caught the cold scent of deeper and deeper recesses. Mme Lecault has been sitting with Mme Berry on the tenth night of a new stretch of insomnia. It is two, two-thirty, but that is only what the clock says. There have been secrets and, as so often when secrets are finally uttered, sudden silences, changes of direction, whether through tact or a fear that walls within walls might be breaking. At some point they have taken different paths, and dozing, drifting in and out of sleep, Mme Lecault catches only occasional fragments of the places Mme Berry's voice would take her. Now it is something about the General and his mess of papers and she wanders off, stepping carefully over them, beginning to tidy what she can in her sudden bottomless exhaustion, dragging each leaf out of darkness, barely able to make out a word, and now, again, it is something about a girl, a poor girl it seems, and history, is it, repeating itself? who has something to do with it may be not the Colonel — was it 'Colonel' she was saying, or 'General'? — but his father who has been so cruel or perhaps it is protected her from someone who *you can not* it is Mme Berry *you can not sit up another minute* and begins to leave and she, Mme Lecault, tries to say something but it does not work and somehow it is next morning, somehow in her own bed, she wakes, another insomnia is over and she wakes and does not even know if she was dreaming.

29

27/v/56

What if one day you stopped writing? By that time, perhaps, I would already have sent you two or three, maybe several never-to-be-answered letters, and I imagine anyway that I would keep doing so. Already I think of these as my lost pages, words I began writing to someone I knew as you but who has now become a desire, a need, something or someone independent and of these pages, whom even you may not recognise, for all your severe and enigmatic answers, your probings. Are they probing because you have reinvented me also? Could that process be traced? Would it be possible to identify a moment when it began, a moment when we started to be other than ourselves? Would it be possible to identify a moment when it was not so?

In my mind you are the person, the only person, I can speak to with absolute honesty; someone out of the world I find myself in, to whom I can communicate free of the constraints of love, of tact, of all these compromises of which it seems every day or hour with others is constructed; someone who will not judge (but is not loving a kind of judgement? and I desire that too!); someone to whom I can bring all my reasons and who will accept not only them but the desires that twist and contort and deflect and insidiously inspire them. The Friend, the Other Half, the Double, the Twin . . . And yet is not that vicious too? Isn't that wishing something of you which at the same time denies you the same? Can we be truly ourselves when we are what another wishes? When we are the other half, the twin of another? Can this be asked?

Can either of us be surprised then, when these letters, their 'you's and 'I's, become a third place, that is between and oblique to us, that is neither of us? (But isn't this also to use them as a cloaca, a drain, a place in which to void ourselves? Isn't there also another need — the need to respond, the need for us not to be ourselves, for us to sacrifice from ourselves — that this need denies? Or are these things somewhere more deeply compatible? The need to escape the boundaries of one's being, to reveal, to utter oneself — mightn't it involve, at last, the giving oneself away? the relinquishment of pride, of boundaries, an abasement that as openly receives as it gives, gives as it receives?)

My God (my god . . .) tell me, is this only myself? And whose answer would I/could I trust? Who can know? And from what level of the great illusion would they speak?

Somewhere, out there, among the stars, you and I, rolling, thrusting, tumbling, joined by the mind, the heart, the teeth. (And yet, for all this, could I enter you again, could I find that place I think I have pushed beyond all reach by the force of my own desiring, I think that the words would spill from me like seed, knowing, being as they can not here, in their feebleness, in this wintry place outside you where however much I arrange them they can only be the ghost, the fetish of what they would truly be.)

30

Bernard turns and fumbles for his watch, knocking over a glass in which there was half an inch of water and so wetting the open pages of the book he had been reading and dampening a corner of his pillow. Cursing, unable to find the watch, he then feels for his glasses and, these also located but knocked from the sidetable and again fumbled for, opened, placed loosely on his nose, switches on his reading-lamp and, squinting against the sudden pain of the light, looks over to the dresser clock. It is 3.06 a.m.

Others are discovering the same thing, or almost. Another clock says 3.03, another 3.10, another 3.07, as is always the case with time. Tad takes longer to wake than most. He turns in his bed, trying to determine whether what he is hearing is a part of the dream — unlikely, since he had been dreaming of eating chocolate — or a part of the other reality, out there in the darkness beyond his window. Eventually — it has only been a matter of a minute or two — he rises, goes to the curtain, and opens it a fraction, very gently. Unbeknown to him until the next afternoon, when he meets Stéphane in the street outside the building, Thérèse and her brother elsewhere on the courtyard are doing the same. And they are not alone.

The strange blue light is filtering again through the upstairs window over at the Ségurs', the usual lamp is on in Mme Lecault's living room, and two or three soft lights have been turned on behind curtained windows in other apartments, but other than these there is little for Tad to see. It is what he hears that is alarming him — that is alarming more and more people in the awakening house. A sobbing, which began very loudly, with something almost like a scream — although at that point, but for the ways it had become already woven into their dreams, almost no one knew that they were hearing it — but now, only a little less loud, has become rhythmical, a chain of long, rasping sounds that soon reaches every corner of the night, every ear in the building, penetrating pillows, hands, blankets, doors locked and curtains drawn against it, as if this — to penetrate, to violate, to break into and break down — were its single, intent purpose.

It continues. No one can sleep. Some — one or two — become angry, or think that they do, and wish that they could shout, yet even these know that this sobbing is somehow not a shouting matter, that it is beyond shouting and probably impermeable to it, that it is somehow beyond things normal and not to be judged by them. Some, back in their beds, stare at the ceiling and, unable as all are to locate its source, allow eventually, unconsciously, the sobbing to take them back into the contours of their own almost-forgotten sorrow. Others, closer to their own pain, begin to weep also or, placing their hands over their ears, or pillows over their heads — finding that the weeping has entered everything and will not be shut out — resign themselves to it as people caught without shelter in a storm resign themselves eventually to rain.

Whether it is a man's or a woman's sobbing is hard to tell. All at first think it a woman's, but as they listen, as their own minds and emotions become soaked with it, it seems to change register, to enter some middle, less definite ground. Perhaps it is a man who has forgotten to cry like a man. Perhaps it is a boy's voice not yet broken. Or perhaps it is just that, the breaking, that confuses them. To some it seems as if there are words amongst the sobs, although they can not clearly make them out or be quite sure of the language. Others, perhaps nearer to the sound, think they hear another, consoling voice, although they too can not be sure. That it is the sound of a heart breaking, that only is clear: or rather, the sound of something like a heart, being torn, being stretched beyond toleration.

No one can tell where it is coming from. To some it seems to come from their neighbours, although it is just as likely, given the acoustics of the courtyard, that it is coming from the neighbour one apartment further down, or from somewhere just above, or just below. Dim lights go on in more of the windows, and other sounds occur — steps on a stairway, a door closing, a woman's muffled voice — but whether these are associated with the sobbing is not clear, and eventually does not matter. Nothing eventually matters, or even makes any difference. In the face of the relentless, inconsolable sobbing, the ordinary world is no more than a thin skin ripped aside to reveal a measureless abyss, a moral-less, norm-less, rule-less void, the vapours rising from which render all who breathe them insensible to matters of the surface. All, in a strange way, feel guilty: no one had known that one could suffer that much. No one had known that here amongst them, invisible, inaudible by day, was a person who could utter so wildly, so openly, so unashamedly what all had somehow always suspected, had somehow always known was there, but had never dared look at, never dared share, for fear that there could then be no returning.

Long after the other lights have gone off, long after even the blue light from the Ségurs' has faded to become almost indistinguishable from the deeper blue of the night, Tad finds that, although the sobbing itself has continued, his own mind has begun to drift from it — whether into sleep or something other would not be easy to tell. For some time now his eyes, although still open, have been seeing not so much the blackness of the courtyard as of some place far within him, so that whether, very near the end of things, it is there, or somewhere here — in the seventh window perhaps, the window that does not exist — that a last light, like a candle guttering, flares for a moment before vanishing becomes accordingly a border issue, a question that, by morning, may not be remembered at all.

At some point the sobbing ceases. Or rather, at some stage, like Tad, each listener finds sleep again, and wakes, one or two or three hours later, to a bright foretaste of approaching summer. M. Bloch, if he could be seen passing Mme Barber on the stairs, would be seen to look at her as if he suspected that it had been she, or perhaps as if he feared that she had found him out. Mme Barber, could she be seen passing M. Bloch, would be found to glance back at him in much the same way. And in truth there would be nothing in those glances to assist even an invisible spectator. Mme Lecault, busy with her window boxes as the tenants drift past, could be seen to look carefully at each, even Bernard, as if for the red eyes, the drawn features that might give them away — finding them, or it, in some, not others, and eventually herself no wiser.

31

It is Sunday. Having spent the morning profitably on the last act of *Richard the Third*, filling the house with Respighi as he did so, the Professor has come downstairs to bring the final ingredients together. He had planned this for the Friday evening, but for that afternoon and most of Saturday (having slept so badly the night before) he was ill and could face no food. Now, however, his appetite has returned, and it is with considerable relish that he stirs in the *chipotle*, places the combs in readiness beside the stove, opens a long-treasured bottle of Chateau Margaux 1934 and, leafing through his favourite recordings, chooses the Villa Lobos.

Soon the sweet, dark mystery of the music, like the rich, cockerel-coloured aroma of the soup, the great opening flower of the wine, fills the room. He sets the table, opens the windows on the late-afternoon sunshine, then, wincing slightly, settles in his chair beside the front curtain, his eyes closed and his feet up on the ancient Lebanese pouffe, waiting for the wine to breathe and for that delicious moment when, at the end of the fifth of the Bachianas, all the instruments having ceased and, unbidden by the printed score, the voice of the soprano rises to a high, high C, two octaves above the middle, and holds the note so long, modulates it so gently toward silence, that you can never be sure that silence has actually arrived, that you can imagine it, this extraordinary note, transcending the human, climbing into some impossible region, never ending.

32

Shit, piss, the smell of rotting vegetables; the acid-brown, hot odour of a squirrel that has died in the roof or rat dead under a cupboard; the smell of Auguste's compost bin, sometimes earthy sweet and sometimes foul: Michael has been working systematically through the senses — at the moment the sense of smell — on the idea that each new thing you experience brings about a feeling you've not had before, and that you are, after all, only the sum of your sensations. The more sensations he has — or so he is inclined to believe — the more of the vast possible him he will have actually discovered.

And what of the other senses? Sight? Taste? Sound?

Taste, it may be, would begin with vegetables — the floury

warmth of potatoes, woody sweetness of carrots, the metallic mustiness of beans, the deep-underground, stone-cellar flavour of cauliflower, broccoli — and lead through pepper, spices, herbs, a hundred fluids from kerosene to beer, vinegar to coffee, blood to the sap of bushes, cognac, curdled milk, to the intense sweetness of chocolate or one of the Greek cakes, steeped in honey, that his father sometimes brings from work; thence to the unexpected sweet-sourness of excrement, the salty thinness of urine, the taste of vomit or bile . . .

It isn't exactly a mortification of the senses, rather the opposite. It is as if they are just waking up, just learning to communicate. With each new smell, each new taste, there is a tiny yet definite expansion of his ability to smell and taste, so that new feelings breed further possibilities, subtler and subtler discriminations, and the only thing that is mortified is the fear of feeling. If the worst that you can smell is vomit or faeces or the stink of rotting flesh or vegetables — what else could there be? — then, for that sense at least, there is not much to be afraid of.

What would be the hardest sense to test in this way? Sight? Not touch. Sight then. The things that one can look upon. It is easier to see than to smell, to taste. Are there things one can not look upon? It's hard to imagine how seeing might actually hurt one — at least, not hurt the eyes themselves (can a vision make the eyes sting?). But is there a different hurting, a hurting not *of*, but *through* the eyes? Is there something more involved with sight? Something moral? Michael's father says that one must not stare, must not turn to look at the elderly man with the great, spongy-skinned growth on his nose, must not look up under women's dresses as they climb the stairs. But if the eyes move in these directions, if these things are there to see, what does it mean that you are not supposed to see them? As if someone has already decided what is ugly, what is hideous. But how could they themselves have decided without looking? Auguste's empty eye socket, the redness and tiny pulse of the vein: is there a reason why you look upon some things with horror, or shock? If you see them too much, will the horror go? Is that why you don't look? But isn't it important that you look? How can you know if you don't? How could it be right, to push the worst things from sight and at the same time to prevent yourself seeing the things your eyes seem most to want to see?

When you lift the lid of Auguste's compost bin in midsummer a cloud of tiny winged insects flies up in your face, along with an almost overpowering stench. If you lift the lid in midwinter the smell is far gentler, though it is still there, and instead of a cloud of tiny midges there are a thousand grey-backed, white-bellied, crescent-shaped grubs around the rim, each one twenty times bigger than a maggot. Michael wonders what they will turn into, if they will turn into anything at all: cabbage moths? Or the soft, black moths that sometimes come in on clothes that have hung out overnight? Or will they perhaps be something else? The sudden thought that the larva of some broad-winged, luminescent blue-and-black butterfly might have been nurtured on the black and slimy putrescence of cabbage leaves, or greeny moulding potato peel, excites as much as it mystifies him.

Once — it was in early spring, when Auguste was preparing a new pumpkin bed — Michael watched him move one of the bins. Underneath it there was a sudden black hole in the grass, a stark, slimy wound. He saw slaters, earthworms, earwigs, slugs, and a dozen other things he couldn't identify, strange, pale creatures that seemed half one thing and half another, never intended to see the light. He imagined shrinking to the size of an ant or grass-mite and moving amongst them, a prehistoric marsh-world full of gigantic, semi-mechanical monsters. Then, as Auguste raked out the bin and began to turn it in with a shovel, there were the lost, forgotten, indissoluble things: an earring, a teaspoon, a small chip of sky-blue china, a grubby cat's eye marble.

Now, revisiting the pumpkin bed — it is a Sunday, late spring — he finds that the long, prickly vines and their giant leaves have taken it over entirely, and the first big pumpkin flowers have appeared, are blaring like great gold-orange trumpets in the late-afternoon light. It seems to Michael that their invisible, inaudible sound is so loud that he has to stop his ears, and clench his knees together, for fear that the pleasure might somehow tear him apart.

33

It is Sunday. Obscurely triumphant, even a little flushed of face, Mme Lecault is standing in the middle of her kitchen with a handful of fresh asparagus. A friend from a small farm across the river, in town to visit her sister, has brought it to her as a spring token, and the concierge is so taken with their freshness, the lush, green-purple, deadly-nightshade pearling of the tips, that she wants to be able to show them to their best advantage. Her only vases are too deep, however, or being used for other things, and the best one for the job was broken months ago. After a few seconds casting about amongst the alternatives she settles upon a small white milk jug, hunts it out, and upends the asparagus into an inch of water, arranging it like a bunch of flowers and leaving it to stand for a moment, while she admires, on the draining-board beside the two cups, the two saucers, the two plates from breakfast. Music is coming in from the courtyard, or rather a fragment of music, a long, high note from the Professor's window, so high and so thin that, having only just paused like this, she has only just now become aware of it (playing yet again as it seems now to be) and is suddenly reminded — such a rich and delicious aroma drifting at the same time from the same apartment — that tonight she might also cook them, and that she will have to decide whether the old way with — was it? — oil and raspberry vinegar? or like the Italians with parmesan cheese, a thin crust of it over the bright steaming green. And still, from outside, winding about the taps and the crockery, the pans and the bowls and the windowsill in the sudden unearthly blue of the kitchen shadows, the long high note repeated and repeated — the soprano hardly pausing for breath — like something that comes from the stars.

Epilogue

FRANCESCO Calvi, did he really do that, or was it a figment of his imagination? Painting a place for himself amongst the angels, then walking in. Reverberate as it may have in the hour of waking, the thought, anyway, disintegrates rapidly in the search for more coffee. Mme Bachelard is two days late. A few last beans help nobody. There is no alternative, for an aged man, but to pick up his stick and walk.

∞

Amongst the tombstones on the hilltop, backlit by sky and high, circling crows — at this time of year it is most likely a newborn lamb dying in the grass — a man is rising from the ground; no easy, miraculous ascent, but slowly, with some difficulty, arthritic. First a head with blue-striped, red woollen cap and pompom, a stubby pipe bowl-downward beneath an overgrown nose. An ancient suede jacket, baggy brown trousers, then, turning, prostrating to an inaudible muezzin, coming up with a long-handled spade. M. Duffy, elder, one of three, he who digs the graves. To skirt him or not is the question. Or to walk straight through: the hole he is digging is right by the path.

'Gaspar. You unsettle me. I thought you were a dead man.'

'Ah. M. Miklus. I don't know. You have come just at the right moment. That is if you would not mind. But I am having trouble pulling the ladder up. When I lift it it falls back against the side and catches on something, a root I think, so that I cannot lift it. I was just about to go back down.'

'If you think an old man can be of any use . . .'

'We are both old, monsieur. I know I am too old for this!'

The two men — Gaspar has put his jacket on the ground, lining upward, so that the other will not soil his trousers — kneel down and try the ladder together. No luck. The gravedigger prepares to descend again, but then, on impulse, Miklus offers to go down instead.

'No, monsieur, you cannot. It is dirty down there.' But the painter insists. If one arthritic man can do it then why not another? After all, how many people get to enter a grave and climb out again?

It is not a root at all, but a stick, or part of a rotten board, a plank, angled downward — it is the angle that is the problem — but pulled out easily enough in that direction. Before ascending, brushing his hands, the painter pauses to look about him. It is much as he might have expected, though at the thought of the board in his hand the flesh suddenly tightens. And then turns upward. Astonishing blue, exactly framed. Cerulean? Lapis lazuli?

Indefinable. Dark, all around it, as if a cinema screen. And then two birds, hard to say how far up. Swallows, the perfect sickles of their wings. No music, in fact no sound at all, but for a moment a colour, a sight almost audible; an urgency, a bright terror within things. *Azure.* And as suddenly the silhouette of a hoary head, light breaking about the pompom.

'Are you going to stay down there forever? Shall I get you a chair?'

∞

A child opens, perhaps the child. Short haired. Taller than he remembers. Huge grey eyes of an owl. Thérèse's. Catherine's. Her sister? But children grow. So many of them a moment, a month, a year there, and then passing, leaving only the images. It is at least a year since he saw her — Isabelle is it? — and then only the once, only briefly. That aura, unearthly: *you must change your life.*

'Hello. Isabelle? Are you Isabelle? Is your mother at home?'

'Yes, . . . and yes, I am Isabelle. Hello monsieur.' Evidently recognising also, though not the same thing. 'Come in.' And by the time he is halfway across the threshold Marie-Louise, red-faced from the kitchen, big with another, and the second — no, third? — clinging to her skirt, barely able yet to stand by itself. Then in the kitchen, at the end of the dark corridor, the second, a girl slightly younger than Isabelle, bred from the same faun. Delicate negotiations. Though perhaps in this case not so difficult, since Marie-Louise herself had modelled for him it must be sixteen years ago. It is the father, Raymond, who may complicate things, but that is the point of coming in the forenoon, to speak with Marie-Louise and leave the matter to her. It is after all an innocuous thing, and he will offer to pay the girl, and to give her one of the sketches. All of them if she wishes.

And then the blessed offer.

'Coffee, yes, please. That would be wonderful. I have come out without mine. In fact I have run out of it. I am on my way to buy some. But first, if I may, I will wash my hands. I have just been helping M. Duffy with something.' And received, I think, a splinter.

Small cottage. Two bedrooms. A tiny, cramped bathroom cluttered with children's things. Bathtoys, miscellaneous plastic parts, caps of shampoo bottles. Generations of soap and hot baths, disinfectants, talc. A splinter, yes, small and dark and too far in to be pinched out.

Good, black, strong, dense, a touch of oil on the meniscus; the first sip clenching the body about it. The long expiration.

The sitting should not be a problem. Marie-Louise laughs at the idea of difficulty with Raymond. Probably he will be only too delighted, especially if Isabelle can be paid a little. But if it could be afternoons and not mornings, and after the end of next week? There are school holidays, and it will be good to have her and Claudine out of each other's hair for a few hours each day.

Then, leaving, another tableau at the doorway. That ache in the fingers. Light, even round the paving stones. Every edge, every colour distinct, every object fathomless. The strange splitting of the self thus, one half retreating into silence while the other waves.

∞

'I've only brought you half the list,' she says as he enters the stone kitchen from the bright morning. There is a cardboard box on the table from which bristle a loaf of bread, leaves of spinach, the top of a soap packet, a carton of eggs. Mme Bachelard is never much given to greetings, though her manner is rather shy than temperamental, and rarely takes more than a few sentences to thaw. 'I think I have everything you will need for the next few days, but if you feel like a walk tomorrow you might get anything I have overlooked.'

'Thank you Pauline. But I'm sure you've thought of everything.' Slightly distant. 'In any case I just went in to the village myself, for coffee. I'm surprised we didn't see each other.'

'Coffee. Oh dear. I've brought some too. But I suppose it's no matter. Coffee will not go stale here.'

'Is there something wrong?' — abrupt, this, but she does seem flushed, distracted, eyes red and rimmed with sleeplessness — 'I expected you yesterday.'

'My father-in-law. He died the night before last.'

'I'm sorry . . . It was inevitable, of course. Tumours of that sort. But I am sorry. Please give Henri my sympathy. His father was an interesting man. I will miss talking to him.'

'He wanted to come home. There was nothing more they could do and they let him come back last week. At least he had a few days out of that place, though I wish we'd had more warning. I'm glad that it didn't last much longer. He was in such pain. It has been very busy, especially this morning. I tried to call you earlier but your telephone is out of order.'

'Oh. No. I've had it off the hook most of the time, at least for the last day or two.'

'You shouldn't do that. You never know who might be trying to reach you.'

'That is the problem. I do know. There aren't many. And I was trying to work.'

'Work! That's good! At last! Who ever heard of a painter who does not paint?'

'It's only been a year, less than that.'

'It's only been less than three years, monsieur, and you have been so irritable.'

'It's been less than a year.' — Smiling — 'What would you know? And who are you to talk of irritable?'

'I must go. I'm sorry. I was going to do a thorough cleaning this week, the place is in such a mess! But it'll have to wait. I am sorry.'

'Please don't even think about it. When is the funeral? I would like to come.'

'That's what we are trying to decide. If you put your telephone back on the hook I will let you know. There's some mail in the box, too,' — she is already halfway out of the door, the spring light in the unruly straw of her hair a golden halo to the skull — 'tucked in the side. I saw the van moving off as I came around the corner below the hill. I thought I might as well bring it up.'

A magazine subscription due for renewal, a note from Claude at the gallery, circulars from the council, and a long letter from Augustine Bernard, the second in as many months, after almost a quarter century.

∞

I am sorry to have made the bones so mysterious. I didn't intend to, but nor did I want to become tiresome by repeating old news. There is certainly no secret about them, at least not from you, although perhaps I should warn you at the outset that, reflecting upon it now, the whole incident seems to me a thing scarcely credible, and that I can only imagine you facing the same disbelief. If that is so, it is so: perhaps we can both regard it as after all this time it must also inevitably be, as a tale sent by one aging artist to another, to put a cosmetic ending to things that might otherwise never have ending at all.

You may remember that around the time of the Professor's death there had been talk of a smell about the place. It did not trouble me particularly. I think I had only the hint of it once or twice and even then it may only have been that others in the house had put me in mind of it. But the matter lingered on. You must have left by the time Mme Lecault decided something had to be done and called in a builder. He nosed about for some time, fattening his bill I suppose, and at last became determined that there were some unusually thick walls or wall-spaces in the building that he was curious about, and he persuaded her to let him investigate further.

This entailed drilling into several walls, even breaking holes in a number of them, and not everyone would allow him. He wished to do something in the Ségurs', for example, and M. Ségur, normally so gentle and obliging, became furious at the suggestion and threatened some sort of legal action. Another of the spaces in question ran alongside Giovanni's old apartment, however, and that being still vacant there could be no real objection. A few bricks were removed from a wall and although nothing that might explain the smell was found, the fact that they did reveal a larger space than one might have expected served only to intensify the search.

A third attempt was made, in the Barbers' apartment. I must admit that to me this had by now become a bit of a goose-chase with no one really knowing what they were doing or why, but Mme Lecault in particular was fixated and prepared to let the builder knock holes through half the house if he were so inclined. Mme Barber, in any case, allowed them to proceed, and a hole was opened to the rear of the ground floor, at the side.

The results were extraordinary, as I can testify myself since I was at home at the time and like several others went over when I heard the commotion. The space uncovered was no larger than that found off the Professor's apartment, indeed it might even have been slightly smaller, but this had clearly been a room or closet of some kind. There was a bed in it, or rather a low wooden bench, upon which were the remnants of a thin horsehair mattress and some bedclothes, and upon these — the point of all this — a skeleton.

It was of a young woman. That is, it seemed to occur almost immediately to those who first saw it that this was the case, given the long black hair still arranged about the skull. And perhaps something else. One would have thought, for example, that it would have been a gruesome spectacle, but somehow it wasn't. Or not so much. There was instead a chilling calm, almost an elegance, as if this after all was the place for such a thing, or it had found its place, although God knows how either could ever have been.

The police were called, of course, and Dr Maurois, since no one could think of who else might advise us. Although it seemed clear that the bones had been there a very long time, and that whatever tragedy they recorded was an old, perhaps even an ancient one, Mme Lecault none the less grew remarkably distraught, began to utter all sorts of strangeness, and I think as much attention was given to calming her as to the discovery itself.

At some point, I think it was because of this attention to Mme Lecault, I found myself alone with the torch and able to look into the space a little more closely than before. Perhaps I was the only one ever able to do so, since it was just a few moments later that the police arrived and in their bumbling inefficiency any possibility of further scrutiny evaporated. But in those moments I thought I saw, and still think I may have seen, something that I do not think anyone else noticed. In the *initial confusion I did not mention it to the police, and when they themselves seemed to have found no such thing I gave up the notion as a figment of my imagination, although I don't say that there might not also have been some scruple in the matter, respect for the dead, I don't know. But in those moments I do think I saw — at the time would have sworn so to the appropriate party had there been one — a second skeleton, albeit the most tenuous, fleeting thing. It may have been a trick of the shadow, of course — it was dark and cramped inside the wall, and the builder had so far removed only bricks enough for someone to lean in rather than scramble through — but there had, for just those few, strange, eerily-calm seconds, seemed to me to be, in the space below the ribs of the larger skeleton, the remains of a far smaller one, a child, a tiny infant, newborn perhaps, or perhaps never born at all.*

But, as I say, there was so little evidence. It may be that the police, who in their haste to widen the hole actually knocked a couple of bricks onto the bench and scattered the bones, had unwittingly destroyed them, for certainly bones so old and delicate would have been fragile indeed and, like the long black hair that seemed to be breaking up even as it was being passed through the hole, might have needed little more than a movement of air, a moment's lack of attention to disintegrate.

In the years since, when I have thought about them — and it's amongst my sins that I've done so less and less — I have explained them to myself in various ways, none of which has ever really satisfied me. It may have been quite simply that what I saw were the remains of a kitten or some other such creature strayed and somehow trapped there much later. Or it might have been more. On a more rarefied level I have even contemplated the possibility that certain things — things perhaps just like this — are created by the strength of the human mind, as visible evidence of some of its more perplexing or less utterable secrets, a sort of confession, although why a child's bones also, and why for me alone to see I could not begin to say.

The police, in any case, took all of this away, and when the press appeared the next day there was nothing but a hole to photograph — I wish I had kept a clipping — and nothing but conjecture with which to garnish the bare facts. Mme Lecault, in any case, was still too disturbed to deal with such attention, and remained so, and we referred any further enquiries to the police who in their turn would say nothing until test results had come from Paris. Which is to presume that the remains ever reached Paris in the first place.

In other words there was a momentary sensation, much speculation, but never anything conclusive. I myself thought the bones could as readily be twenty or fifty as a hundred years old, and hoped that the final forensic reports would give some indication, but if they ever arrived I did not hear of them. All I heard, and I think all anyone else in the apartments ever heard, was that the police had found no case the bones could very readily be attached to, and did not propose to pursue the matter further.

I've always thought it unfortunate that the young woman and her child, if child it was, were ever disturbed at all. Certainly Mme Lecault never properly recovered, and the Barbers left rather than stay on in the building. The strange final irony is that the builder had at last to admit that all of this had nothing to do with the smell that had set him looking in the first place. The smell — apparently, for I never again caught a trace of it myself — continued to hang about in much the same niggling and elusive manner as before, then after a few months went away of its own accord.

Clearly it all defied logic, but as clearly logic had very little to do with it. You would think that the room or closet itself might have offered a clue, but there was certainly none that I could see. There was no concealed door, no bricked-up window, and I suspect even the ceiling, had anyone thought to have broken into it, would have revealed only a couple of centuries of mortar dust, rat-droppings and spider webs if it did not actually, as was most likely, open on to the underside of Giovanni's study floor. Certainly nothing to substantiate the lingering feeling I have had ever since, as furtive and stubborn as the smell itself, that this entire phenomenon, sombre enough on its own, hovered on the edge of some further darkness: that it was not so much that this young woman had been walled in and died, evident as it was that some such thing had been the case, but that she had been, and perhaps was still, guarding something or, stranger yet, waiting, outside something, to be let in. That she was somehow in two places at once, and that, had we actually gone ahead and broken down another of the walls surrounding her, we might have found ourselves staring out at another house entirely.

∽

A hum somewhere, far off, all about, that may be a million bees but is perhaps only or also the drone of the day, movements of air, running water, the sound of a car between Mis and Arduille. A fly mizzles in a corner of the window, thwarted by glass. Isabelle blinks, moves her fingers on the book's spine — it is *Wuthering Heights* — absorbed in something going on there, fields, horses, pages within the page, her head still turned to catch light from the window, its whiteness heightened by hers, huge eyes opaque, a scratch of chalk, or alabaster, suggesting the iris. Stroke by stroke thus a place opening, space for a person to continue, for the form, the shape of her to stay while the rest rises, goes down to lunch, moves off into the rest of her life. He clears his throat, turns from the easel to find a nail, the end of a brush to make the scratch with, turns back to recheck the fall of shadow from a skirt-fold, calculating the risk of another brushstroke, worrying instead the stuccoed wall.

In which place, that or this, does the air stir faintly from their lips, the warmth and scent of their bodies form a coast, a nimbus about them? He steps back, slightly, to survey it whole. Isabelle, in green tights and lemon smock, kneeling at the pink chair, her elbows on the hard seat cushioned by the old brown jacket, reading a tall blue book. Behind her a white chair drawn up to the paint-spattered table, a bowl of fruit (a pear, an apple), a box of her favourite biscuits. And, tall, at the window behind her, holding the curtain aside, his own back toward him (the difficulty, that, of being oneself and not, of being *here* painting oneself *there*), a slab of dark, mottled green to offset the wide whiteness of the window.

So much; though there are also the stone flagon, the stepladder, the intentional scuff on the other side, by the white chair, as of paint flaked from a fresco, the work thus indicating itself as painting only, pointing the irony that in staring out of the wide, white window we are also staring inward, the sky before us — before him — with its darting swallows, its flock of high cloud, also the canvas, also a wall, the place where the stone of it most nearly breaks through. As if a word, a step, a brushstroke might take him to the heart of things — or one last flourish of the pen of someone who, stubbing out her cigarette, stretching her long legs before her, now rises, moves to the window, throws open the curtains at last.